AT NIGHT ALL BLOOD IS BLACK

AT
NIGHT
ALL
BLOOD
IS
BLACK

DAVID DIOP

Translated from the French by Anna Moschovakis

FARRAR, STRAUS AND GIROUX   III   NEW YORK

Farrar, Straus and Giroux
120 Broadway, New York 10271

Printed in the United States of America
Originally published in French in 2018 by Éditions du Seuil,
    France, as *Frère d'âme*
English translation published in the United States by Farrar,
    Straus and Giroux
First American edition, 2020

Library of Congress Cataloging-in-Publication Data
Names: Diop, David, 1966– author. | Moschovakis, Anna,
    translator.
Title: At night all blood is black / David Diop ; translated from
    the French by Anna Moschovakis.
Other titles: Frère d'âme. English
Description: First American edition. | New York : Farrar, Straus
    and Giroux, 2020.
Identifiers: LCCN 2020013691 | ISBN 9780374266974
    (hardcover)
Classification: LCC PQ3989.2.D563 F7413 2020 |
    DDC 843/.914—dc23
LC record available at https://lccn.loc.gov/2020013691

Designed by Richard Oriolo

Our books may be purchased in bulk for promotional,
educational, or business use. Please contact your local
bookseller or the Macmillan Corporate and Premium Sales
Department at 1-800-221-7945, extension 5442, or by e-mail at
MacmillanSpecialMarkets@macmillan.com.

www.fsgbooks.com
www.twitter.com/fsgbooks • www.facebook.com/fsgbooks

10   9   8   7   6   5   4   3   2   1

For my first reader, my wife,
eyes bathed in clearest light;
three black gems smile in your irises.
For my children like the fingers on a hand.
For my parents, bearers of this métisse life.

We embraced each other by our names.

—Montaigne, "Of Friendship"

Who thinks, betrays.

—Pascal Quignard, *Mourir de penser*

I am two simultaneous voices, one long, the other short.

—Cheikh Hamidou Kane, *Ambiguous Adventure*

AT NIGHT ALL BLOOD IS BLACK

I ₁₁₁

. . . **I KNOW, I UNDERSTAND,** I shouldn't have done it. I, Alfa Ndiaye, son of the old, old man, I understand, I shouldn't have. God's truth, now I know. My thoughts belong to me alone, I can think what I want. But I won't tell. The ones I might have told my secret thoughts to, my brothers-in-arms who will be left so disfigured, maimed, eviscerated, that God will be ashamed to see them show up in Paradise and the Devil will be happy to welcome them to

Hell, will never know who I really am. The survivors won't know a thing, my old father won't know, and my mother, if she is still of this world, will never find out. The weight of shame will not be added to the weight of my death. They won't imagine what I've thought, what I've done, the depths to which the war drove me. God's truth, the family honor will be spared, the honor of appearances.

I know, I understand, I shouldn't have. In the world before, I wouldn't have dared, but in today's world, God's truth, I allow myself the unthinkable. No voice rises in my head to forbid me: my ancestors' voices and my parents' voices all extinguished themselves the minute I conceived of doing what, finally, I did. I know now, I swear to you that I understood it fully the moment I realized that I could think anything. It happened like that, all of a sudden without warning, it hit me brutally in the head, like a giant seed of war dropped from the metallic sky, the day Mademba Diop died.

Ah! Mademba Diop, my more-than-brother, took too long to die. It was very, very difficult, it wouldn't end, from dawn into evening, his guts in the air, his insides outside, like a sheep that has been ritually dismembered after the sacrifice. Except Mademba was not yet dead, and already the insides of his body were outside. While the others hid in the gaping wounds in the earth we called trenches, I stayed close to Mademba, I lay pressed against him, my right hand in his left hand, staring at the cold blue sky crisscrossed with metal. Three times he asked me to finish him off, three times I refused. This was before, before I allowed myself to think anything I want. If I had been then what I've become today, I would have killed him the first time he asked, his head turned toward me, his left hand in my right.

God's truth, if I'd already become then what I am now, I would have slaughtered him like a sacrificial sheep, out of friendship. But I thought of my old father, of my mother, of the inner voice that commands us all, and I couldn't cut the barbed wire of his suffering. I was not humane with Mademba, my more-than-brother, my childhood friend. I let duty make my choice. I offered him only mistaken thoughts, thoughts commanded by duty, thoughts condoned by a respect for human law, and I was not human.

God's truth, I let Mademba cry like a small child, the third time he begged me to finish him off, pissing himself, his right hand groping at the ground to gather his scattered guts, slimy as freshwater snakes. He said to me, "By the grace of God and of our marabout, if you are my brother, Alfa, if you are really who I think you are, slit my throat like a sacrificial sheep, don't let the scavengers of death devour my body! Don't abandon me to all that filth. Alfa Ndiaye . . . Alfa . . . I'm begging you . . . slit my throat!"

But precisely because he spoke to me of our great marabout, precisely so as not to disobey the laws of humanity, the laws of our ancestors, I was not humane and I let Mademba, my more-than-brother, my childhood friend, die with his eyes full of tears, his hand trembling, groping the muddy battlefield for his guts so he could stuff them back into his open belly.

Ah, Mademba Diop! Only after you were gone did I finally begin to think. Only with your death, at dusk, did I know, did I understand that I would no longer listen to the voice of duty, the voice that commands, the voice that leads the way. But it was too late.

Once you were dead, your hands finally immobile, finally at rest, finally released from their shameful suffering by your last breath, I thought only that I should not have waited. I understood, one breath too late, that I should have slit your throat as soon as you asked me to, while your eyes were still dry, your left hand clasped in mine. I shouldn't have let you suffer like an old solitary lion, eaten alive by hyenas, its insides turned out. I let you plead with me for reasons that were corrupt, because of thoughts that arrived fully formed, too well dressed to be honest.

Ah, Mademba! How I've regretted not killing you on the morning of the battle, while you were still asking me nicely, as a friend, with a smile in your voice! To have slit your throat in that moment would have been the last good bit of fun I could have given you in your life, a way to stay friends for eternity. But instead of coming through for you, I let you die condemning me, bawling, drooling, screaming, shitting yourself like a feral child. In the name of who knows what human laws, I abandoned you to your miserable lot. Maybe to save my own soul, maybe to remain the person those who raised me hoped for me to be, before God and before man. But before you, Mademba, I was incapable of being a man. I let you curse me, my friend, you, my more-than-brother, I let you scream, blaspheme, because I did not yet know how to think for myself.

But as soon as you were dead, with a final groan, your guts exposed, my friend, my more-than-brother, as soon as you were dead, I knew, I understood that I should not have abandoned you.

I waited a bit, stretched out next to your remains, and stared at the night sky, deepest blue blue, crisscrossed by the sparkling trails of the last tracer bullets. And as soon as silence fell on the blood-soaked battlefield, I began to think. You were no more than a heap of dead meat.

I set about doing what you hadn't managed to do all day because your hand was too unsteady. I neatly gathered your still-warm guts and deposited them into your belly, as if into a sacred vessel. In the twilight, I thought I saw you smile at me and I decided to take you home. In the cold of night, I took off my regulation trench coat and my shirt. I slid my shirt onto your body and tied the sleeves against your stomach, a very, very tight double knot that became stained with your black blood. I picked you up and brought you back to the trench. I held you in my arms like a child, my more-than-brother, my friend, and I walked and walked in the mud, in the crevices carved out by mortar shells, filled with blood-stained water, dispersing the rats that had left their burrows to feed on human flesh. And as I carried you in my arms, I began to think for myself, by asking your forgiveness. I knew, I understood too late what I should have done when you asked me, eyes dry, the way one asks a favor of a childhood friend, like a debt owed, without ceremony, sweetly. Forgive me.

II ₌₌₌

I WALKED FOR A LONG TIME through the fissures in the earth, carrying Mademba, heavy like a sleeping child, in my arms. An enemy target escaping notice under the light of the full moon, I arrived at the gaping hole that was our trench. Seen from a distance, our trench looked to me like the slightly parted lips of an immense woman's sex. A woman, open, offering herself to war, to the bombshells, and to us, the soldiers. It was the first unmentionable thing I allowed myself to think. Before Mademba's death, I would never have dared imagine such a thing, would never have thought of the trench as an outsized female organ ready to receive us, Mademba and me. The insides of the earth were outside, the insides of my mind were outside, and I knew, I understood that I could think anything I wanted to, on the condition that the others knew nothing of it. So I locked my thoughts back in my head after observing them from up close. Strange.

The others welcomed me to the belly of the earth like a hero. I'd walked beneath the bright moon, my arms around Mademba, without seeing that a long ribbon of his intestine had escaped from my shirt knotted around his waist. When they saw the human disaster I was carrying in my arms, they said I was courageous and strong. They said they would not have been able to do it. That they might have abandoned Mademba Diop to the rats, that they wouldn't have dared to neatly gather his guts into the sacred vessel of his body. They said that they would not have carried him such a long distance beneath such a bright moon in sight of, and with the knowledge of, the enemy. They said I deserved a medal, that I would be given the Croix de Guerre, that my family would be proud of me, that Mademba, looking down on me from the sky, would be proud of me. Even our General Mangin would be proud of me. And yet I was thinking that I didn't care about the medal, though no one would ever know this. Like no one would ever know that Mademba had begged me three times to finish him, that I had remained deaf to his three supplications, that I had been inhuman by obeying duty's voice. But I was now free to listen no longer, to no longer obey the voices that command us not to be human when we must.

III ₃

IN THE TRENCH, I lived like the others, I drank, I ate like the others. Sometimes I sang, like the others. I sing off-key and everyone laughed when I sang. They would say, "You Ndiayes, you can't sing." They made fun of me, a little, but they respected me. They didn't know what I thought of them. I found them foolish, I found them idiotic, because they didn't think about anything. Soldiers, black or white, who always say "yes." When commanded to leave the shelter of their trench to attack the enemy, defenseless, it's "yes."

When told to play the savage, to scare off the enemy, it's "yes." The captain told them that the enemy was afraid of savage Negroes, cannibals, Zulus, and they laughed. They're content if the enemy on the other side is afraid of them. They're content to forget their own fear. So when they leap from the trench, their rifles in their left hands and their machetes in their right, hurling themselves out of the earth's belly, they do so with eyes like madmen. The captain has told them they are great warriors, so they love to get themselves killed while singing, so their madness becomes a competition. A Diop would not want it said of him that he is less courageous than a Ndiaye, and so the minute the sound of Captain Armand's whistle commands him, he leaps up from his hole and screams like a savage. Same rivalry between the Keïtas and the Soumarés. Same thing between the Diallos and the Fayes, the Kanes and the Thiounes, the Dianés, the Kouroumas, the Bèyes, the Fakolis, the Salls, the Diengs, the Secks, the Kas, the Cissés, the Ndours, the Tourés, the Camaras, the Bas, the Falls, the Coulibalys, the Sonkhos, the Sys, the Cissokhos, the Dramés, the Traorés. They will all die without thinking because Captain Armand has said to them, "You, the Chocolats of black Africa, are naturally the bravest of the brave. France admires you and is grateful. The papers talk only of your exploits!" So they love to sprint onto the battlefield to be beautifully massacred while screaming like madmen, regulation rifle in the left hand and savage machete in the right.

But I, Alfa Ndiaye, I understand the true meaning of the captain's words. No one knows what I think. I am free to think whatever I want. And what I think is that people don't want me to think. The unthinkable is what is hidden behind the captain's words. The captain's France needs for us to play the savage when it suits them. They need for us to be savage because the enemy is afraid of our machetes. I know, I understand, it's no more complicated than that. The captain's France needs our savagery, and because we are obedient, myself and the others, we play the savage. We slash the enemy's flesh, we maim, we decapitate, we disembowel. The only difference between my friends the Toucouleurs and the Sérères, the Bambaras and the Malinkés, the Soussous, the Haoussas, the Mossis, the Markas, the Soninkés, the Senoufos, the Bobos, and the other Wolofs, the only difference between them and me is that I became savage intentionally. They play a role only when they crawl out from the earth, but I play a role only with them, inside our sheltering trench. In their company, I laughed and I even sang off-key, but they respected me.

As soon as I left the trench sprinting, as soon as the trench birthed me and I began to scream, the enemy was in trouble. I never retreated when a retreat was called, I would return to the trench in my own time. The captain knew this, he let it happen, amazed when I would return each time alive, smiling. He let it happen, even when I returned late, because I would bring trophies back to the trench. I brought back the spoils of a savage war. I brought back, at the end of every battle, in the dark night or in the night bathed in moonlight and blood, an enemy rifle, along with the hand that went with it. The hand that had carried it, the hand that had gripped it, the hand that had cleaned it, discharged it, and reloaded it. So when the retreat was sounded, the captain and my trench-mates who had come back to bury themselves alive in the damp protection of our trench asked themselves questions. First: "Will Alfa Ndiaye come back to us alive?" Second: "Will Alfa Ndiaye come back with an enemy rifle and the hand that carried it?" And I always came back to the earth's womb after the others, sometimes under enemy fire, whether it was windy or raining or snowing, as the captain said. And I always brought an enemy rifle and the hand that had carried it, gripped it, cleaned it, greased it, the hand that had loaded it, discharged it, and reloaded it. And the captain and my surviving trench-mates who always asked themselves those two questions on the evenings of attacks were pleased when they heard shots and enemy cries. They would say to each other, "Well, Alfa Ndiaye must be on his way home. But will he bring back a rifle and the severed hand that goes with it?" A rifle, a hand.

Home with my trophies, I saw that they were very, very pleased with me. They saved food for me, they saved bits of tobacco. They were truly so pleased to see me come back that they never asked me how I did it, how I captured the enemy rifle and the severed hand. They were so pleased that I'd come back because they liked me. I had become their totem. The hands confirmed for them that they were still alive for one more day. Nor did they ever ask me what I had done with the rest of the body. How I had captured the enemy, that didn't interest them. Nor how I'd cut off the hand. What interested them was the result, the savagery. And they laughed with me, thinking that for some time now the enemies on the other side must be very, very afraid, imagining their own hands being severed. And still, my captain and my trench-mates didn't know how I captured them and what I did with the rest of their bodies after. They couldn't imagine even a fraction of a fraction of what I did to the bodies, they couldn't imagine even a fraction of the fear felt by the enemies on the other side.

When I leave the belly of the earth, I am inhuman by choice, I become a little inhuman. Not because the captain commanded me to, but because I have thought it and willed it. When I leap, shrieking, from the earth's womb, I do not intend to kill multiple enemies from the other side, but to kill just one, in my own way, calmly, deliberately, slowly. When I emerge from the earth, my rifle in my left hand

and my machete in my right, I'm not concerned about my trench-mates. I don't know them anymore. They fall around me, faces in the soil, one by one, and I run, I shoot, and I throw myself flat on my stomach. I run, I shoot, and I crawl under the barbed wire. While shooting, I might kill an enemy by accident, without really meaning to. I might. But what I want is to fight face-to-face. That's why I run, shoot, throw myself on my stomach and crawl, to arrive as close as possible to the enemy on the other side. In sight of their trench, I slow to a crawl, then, little by little, I stop moving almost completely. I play dead. I wait, calmly, to capture one of them. I wait until one comes out of his hole. I wait for the evening cease-fire, the moment of relief, when the shooting stops.

One always comes out from a mortar-shell hole where he's taken refuge until he can return to his trench close to dusk, when no one is shooting. Then, with my machete, I slash the backs of his knees. It's easy, he thinks I'm dead. The enemy from the other side doesn't see me, a corpse among corpses. Now, in his mind, I've come back from the dead to kill him. The enemy from the other side is so scared, he doesn't make a sound when I slash the backs of his knees. He just crumples. So I disarm him, then I gag him. I tie his hands behind his back.

Sometimes it's easy. Sometimes it's more difficult. Some of them don't give in. Some don't want to believe that they're going to die. Some resist. So I knock them out, silently, because I'm twenty years old and, as the captain says, a force of nature. Then I pick them up either by the sleeve of their uniform or by a boot, and I pull them very gently as I crawl into la terre à personne, "no-man's-land," as the captain says, between the two giant trenches, across the mortar holes, across the pools of blood. Whether it's wind, rain, sleet, or snow, as the captain says, I wait for him to wake up, I wait patiently for the enemy from the other side to wake up if I've knocked him out. If I don't have to knock him out, if the one I dragged from his mortar-shell hole has let me take him, believing he can outsmart me, I wait and catch my breath. I wait until we're both calm. While waiting, I smile at him, in the light of the moon and the stars, so he doesn't become too agitated. But when I smile at him, I can sense him wondering, "What does this savage want from me? Is he going to eat me? Is he going to rape me?" I am free to imagine what the enemy from the other side thinks because I know, I understand. Looking into the enemy's blue eyes, I often see a panicked fear of death, of savagery, of rape, of cannibalism. I see in his eyes what he's been told about me, and what he's believed without ever seeing me. I think that in seeing me look at him, smiling, he's telling himself that they didn't lie to him, that with my teeth, white at night with or without a moon, I will devour him alive, or something even worse.

The terrible thing is when, once I've caught my breath,

I undress the enemy from the other side. When I unbutton the top of his uniform, that's when I see the enemy's blue eyes mist up. That's when I sense that he fears the worst. Whether he's stoic or distraught, brave or cowardly, at the moment I unbutton the jacket of his uniform, then the shirt, to expose his belly, bright white in the moonlight or in the rain or in the softly falling snow, that's when I catch the eyes of the enemy from the other side starting to dim. They're all the same, the tall ones, the short ones, the fat ones, the brave ones, the cowardly ones, the proud ones, when they see me looking at their trembling white bellies, their eyes go dim. All the same.

Then I pull back a little and I think about Mademba Diop. And each time I hear him in my head begging me to slit his throat and I think that I was inhuman enough to let him beg me three times. What I didn't do for my friend I can do for my enemy. Out of humanity.

When they see me reach for my machete, the blue eyes of the enemy from the other side extinguish themselves for good. The first time, the enemy kicked me and tried to run away. Since then, I make sure to bind the ankles of the enemy from the other side. And that's why, as soon as I have my machete in my right hand, the enemy starts to squirm like a madman, as if he thinks he can escape. It's impossible. The enemy from the other side must know that he can no longer escape, being so tightly bound, but still he hopes. I can read it in his blue eyes the way I read it in Mademba Diop's black eyes, the hope that I might alleviate his suffering.

His white belly is exposed, it rises and falls in jerks. The enemy from the other side gasps and screams, now in stark silence because of the gag I've cinched around his mouth. He screams in stark silence when I take all the insides of his belly and put them outside in the rain, in the wind, in the snow, or in the bright moonlight. If at this moment his blue eyes don't dim forever, then I lie down next to him, I turn his face toward mine and I watch him die a little, then I slit his throat, cleanly, humanely. At night, all blood is black.

IV_{III}

GOD'S TRUTH, on the day of his death it took me no time to find Mademba Diop, disemboweled on the battlefield. I know, I understand what happened. Mademba told me, before his hands began trembling, while he was still asking me nicely, as a friend, to finish him off.

He was in the middle of a full-blown attack against the enemy on the other side, gun in his left hand and machete in his right, his performance was in full swing, he was fully playing the savage, when he fell upon an enemy from the other side who was pretending to be dead. Mademba Diop leaned in to look, casually, in passing, before moving on. He stopped to look at a dead enemy who was only pretending. He stared at him because, even still, he had his doubts. A brief instant. The face of the enemy from the other side wasn't gray like the faces of dead people, white or black. This one looked like it was playing dead. Take no prisoners, finish him with the machete, Mademba thought. Don't let down your guard. Kill this half-dead enemy from the other side a second time, just to be safe, so as never to have to feel bad about one of your brothers-in-arms, one of your friends, taking the same route and getting caught.

And while he is thinking about his brothers-in-arms, about his friends, whom he must protect from this half-dead enemy, while he pictures this half-dead enemy dealing a blow to someone other than himself, maybe to me, his more-than-brother, who may as well be him, while he's telling himself that he must be vigilant for others, he's not being vigilant for himself. Mademba told me, sweetly, as a friend, still smiling, that the enemy had opened his eyes wide before tearing open Mademba's stomach from top to bottom in a single slash with the bayonet he'd held hidden in his right hand beneath a fold of his big coat. Mademba, still smiling about the half-dead enemy's attack on him, told me calmly that there was nothing he could have done. He told me this at the beginning, when he wasn't yet suffering so much, not long before his first plea to, as his friend, finish him off. His first plea addressed to me, his more-than-brother, Alfa Ndiaye, youngest son of the old man.

Before Mademba could react, before he could take revenge, the enemy, who still had some life in him, fled back to his line. Between his first and second pleas, I asked Mademba to describe the enemy from the other side who had disemboweled him. "He has blue eyes," Mademba murmured, as I lay by his side looking at the sky crisscrossed with metal. I asked again. "God's truth, all I can tell you is that he had blue eyes." I asked again and again: "Is he tall, is he short? Is he good-looking, is he ugly?" And Mademba Diop, each time, responded that it wasn't the enemy from the other side I should kill, that it was too late, that the enemy had had the good luck to survive. The person I now had to kill a second time, to finish off, was him, Mademba.

But, God's truth, I didn't really listen to Mademba, my childhood friend, my more-than-brother. God's truth, I thought only of gutting the half-dead blue-eyed enemy. I thought only of disemboweling the enemy from the other side, and I neglected my own Mademba Diop. I listened to the voice of vengeance. I was inhuman from the moment of Mademba Diop's second plea, when he said, "Forget the blue-eyed enemy. Kill me now because I'm suffering too much. We're the same age, we were circumcised on the same day. You lived at my house, I watched you grow up and you watched me. Because of that, you can make fun of me, I can cry in front of you, I can ask you anything. We are more than brothers because we chose each other as brothers. Please, Alfa, don't let me die like this, my guts in the air, my stomach devoured by a gnawing pain. I don't know if the blue-eyed enemy is tall, if he's short, if he's good-looking, or if he's ugly. I don't know if he's young like us or if he's our fathers' age. He was lucky, he saved himself. He is no longer important. If you are my brother, my childhood friend, if you are the one I have always known, the one I love like I love my mother and my father, then I beg you a second time to slit my throat. Do you enjoy hearing me moan like a little boy? Watching as my dignity is chased away by shame?"

But I refused. Ah! I refused. I'm sorry, Mademba Diop, I'm sorry, my friend, my more-than-brother, not to have listened to you with my heart. I know, I understand, I shouldn't have turned my mind toward the blue-eyed enemy from the other side. I know, I understand, I shouldn't have been thinking about the vengeance demanded by my brain, furrowed by your tears, seeded by your cries, when you weren't even dead yet. But I heard a powerful and commanding voice that forced me to ignore your suffering. "Do not kill your best friend, your more-than-brother. It isn't for you to take his life. Don't mistake yourself for the hand of God. Don't mistake yourself for the hand of the Devil.

Alfa Ndiaye, could you stand before Mademba's father and mother knowing that it was you who killed him, that it was you who finished the work of the blue-eyed enemy?"

No, I know, I understand, I shouldn't have listened to the voice that exploded in my head. I should have shut it up while there was still time. I should already have been thinking for myself. I should, Mademba, have finished you off out of friendship so that you would stop weeping, writhing, contorting yourself in an effort to put back into your belly what had come out of it and was sucking at the air like a freshly caught fish.

V_{III}

GOD'S TRUTH, I WAS INHUMAN. I didn't listen to my friend, I listened to my enemy. So when I capture the enemy from the other side, when I read in his blue eyes the screams his mouth can't sling into the skies of war, when his open belly has become nothing more than a pulp of raw flesh, I turn back the clock, I finish off the enemy. As soon as he's made a second plea with his eyes, I slit his throat like a sacrificial lamb. What I didn't do for Mademba Diop, I do for my blue-eyed enemy. Out of my reclaimed humanity.

And then I take his rifle, after cutting off his right hand with my machete. It takes a long time and is very, very difficult. When I crawl home, slipping under barbed wire, between wooden posts rising from the viscous mud, when I come home to our trench that's spread open like a woman facing the sky, I'm covered with the blood of the enemy from the other side. I'm like a statue made of mud and blood mixed together and I stink so badly even the rats flee.

My stench is the stench of death. Death has the stench of the inside of the body turned outside its sacred vessel. In the open air, the inside of the body of any human being or animal becomes corrupted. From the richest man to the poorest, from the most beautiful woman to the ugliest, from the most feral animal to the most harmless, from the most powerful to the weakest. Death is the stench of the decomposed inside of the body, and even the rats are afraid when they smell me coming, crawling beneath the barbed wire. They dread the sight of death moving, advancing toward them, so they flee. They flee at home in the trench, too, even after I wash my body and my clothes, even when I think I've purified myself.

VI.

MY TRENCH-MATES, my war brothers, began to fear me after the fourth hand. At first, they laughed with me heartily, they enjoyed watching me come home with a rifle and an enemy hand. They were so pleased with me, they even thought of giving me another medal. But after the fourth enemy hand, they no longer laughed so easily. The white soldiers were beginning to say—I could read it in their eyes—"This Chocolat is really strange." The others, Chocolat soldiers from West Africa like me, began to say—and I also read it in their eyes—"This Alfa Ndiaye from the village of Gandiol near Saint-Louis in Senegal is strange. When did he become so strange?"

The Toubabs and the Chocolats, as the captain called them, continued to slap me on the shoulder, but their laughter and their smiles had changed. They began to be very, very, very afraid of me. They began to whisper, right after the fourth enemy hand.

For the first three hands I was a legend, they cheered me when I returned, they fed me delicacies, offered me tobacco, helped me rinse off with big buckets of water, helped me clean my uniform. I saw in their eyes that they understood. I was performing, in their place, the grotesque savage, the enlisted savage obeying orders. The enemy on the other side should be trembling in his boots and under his helmet.

In the beginning, my war brothers weren't bothered by my stench of death, the stench of a butcher of human flesh, but beginning with the fourth hand they avoided smelling me. They continued to give me delicacies, to offer me bits of tobacco they'd collected from here or there, to lend me a blanket to warm myself, but with a fake smile plastered on their terrified soldiers' faces. They no longer helped me rinse myself with big buckets. They let me clean my uniform myself. Suddenly, nobody was slapping me on the shoulder and laughing. God's truth, I became untouchable.

So they set aside a bowl, a cup, a fork, and a spoon for me

that they kept in a corner of our dugout. When I came home very late at night on battle days, long after the others, never mind the wind, rain, or snow, as the captain said, the cook would tell me to go get my things. When he served me soup, he was very, very careful that his ladle not touch the interior, the sides, or the rim of my bowl.

The rumor spread. It spread, and as it spread it shed its clothes and, eventually, its shame. Well dressed at the beginning, well appointed at the beginning, well outfitted, well medaled, the brazen rumor ended up with her legs spread, her ass in the air. I didn't notice it right away, I didn't recognize the change, I didn't know what she was plotting. Everyone had seen her but no one described her to me. I finally caught wind of the whispers and learned that my strangeness had been transformed into madness, and madness into witchcraft. Soldier sorcerer.

Don't tell me that we don't need madness on the battlefield. God's truth, the mad fear nothing. The others, white or black, play at being mad, perform madness so that they can calmly throw themselves in front of the bullets of the enemy on the other side. It allows them to run straight at death without being too afraid. You'd have to be mad to obey Captain Armand when he whistles for the attack, knowing there's almost no chance you'll come home alive. God's truth, you'd have to be crazy to drag yourself screaming out of the belly of the earth. The bullets from the enemy on the other side, the giant seeds falling from the metallic sky, they aren't afraid of screams, they aren't afraid to pass through heads, flesh, to break bones and to sever lives. Temporary madness makes it possible to forget the truth about bullets. Temporary madness, in war, is bravery's sister.

But when you seem crazy all the time, continuously, without stopping, that's when you make people afraid, even your war brothers. And that's when you stop being the brave one, the death-defier, and become instead the true friend of death, its accomplice, its more-than-brother.

VII <small>III</small>

FOR EVERYONE, for the soldiers both black and white, I have become death. I know this, I understand. Whether Toubab soldiers or Chocolat soldiers like me, they think I'm a sorcerer, a devourer of people's insides, a dëmm. They think I've always been one, but that the war has revealed it. The rumor, stark naked now, claimed I had eaten the insides of Mademba Diop, my more-than-brother, before he was even dead. The brazen rumor said that I should be feared. The rumor, spread-legged and ass in air, said that I devoured the insides of the enemies from the other side, but also the insides of friends. The obscene rumor said, "Beware, watch out. What does he do with the severed hands? He shows them to us and then they disappear. Beware, watch out."

God's truth, I, Alfa Ndiaye, youngest child of the old man, saw the rumor chase after me, half-naked, shameless, like a fallen woman. And yet the Toubabs and the Chocolats who watched the rumor chase me, who lifted her skirt as she passed, who pinched her ass, snickering, continued to smile at me, to talk to me as if nothing was wrong, friendly on the outside but terrorized on the inside, even the toughest, even the hardest, even the bravest.

When the captain whistled for us to surge out of the belly of the earth so that we could throw ourselves like savages, temporary madmen, on the enemy's little iron seeds that were oblivious to our shrieks, nobody would take their place beside me. No one would dare rub shoulders with me anymore in the cacophony of war, leaping from the earth's hot entrails. No one wanted to be next to me when they fell to the bullets from the other side. God's truth, now I was in the war alone.

That's how the enemy hands earned me my solitude, beginning with the fourth. Solitude in the midst of smiles, winks, encouragement from my trench-mates, black or white. God's truth, nobody wanted to attract the evil eye of a soldier sorcerer, the shit luck of death's best friend. I know this, I understand. They don't think much, but when they think, they think in dualistic terms. I've read it in their eyes. They think devourers of human insides are good so long as they devour only the enemy's insides. But devourers of souls are no good when they eat the insides of their trench-mates. With soldier sorcerers, you never know. My trench-mates believe they have to be very, very careful with soldier sorcerers, they have to manage them carefully, to smile, to be friendly, to talk casually to them about this and that, but from afar, never to approach them, touch them, brush against them, or it's certain death, it's the end.

It's why, after the first few hands, whenever Captain Armand whistled for the attack, they kept themselves ten large steps away from either side of me. Some of them, just before they would leap screaming from the earth's hot entrails, would avoid even looking at me, letting their eyes fall on me, glancing at me at all, as if to look at me was to touch the face, arms, hands, back, ears, legs of death. As if to look at me was to die.

Humans are always finding absurd explanations for things. I know this, I understand it, now that I'm able to think what I want. My brothers in combat, white or black, need to believe that it isn't the war that will kill them, but the evil eye. They need to believe that it won't be one of the thousands of bullets fired by the enemy from the other side that will randomly kill them. They don't like randomness.

Randomness is too absurd. They want someone to blame, they'd rather think that the enemy bullet that hits them was directed, guided by someone cruel, malevolent, with evil intent. They believe that this cruel, malevolent, evil-intentioned one is me. God's truth, their thinking is weak, flimsy. They think that if I'm alive after all these attacks, if no bullet has hit me, it's because I'm a soldier sorcerer. They think the worst. They say that many of their trench-mates have been hit by bullets that were meant for me.

This is why some of them smiled hypocritically at me. It's why others looked away when I appeared, why still others closed their eyes to keep them from falling on me, from grazing me. I became taboo, like a totem.

The totem of the Diops, of Mademba Diop, that egotist, is a peacock. He said "peacock" and I replied "crowned crane." I said, "Your totem is a fowl, while mine is a wildcat. The Ndiayes' totem is the lion, it's nobler than the totem of the Diops." I let myself repeat to my more-than-brother Mademba Diop that his totem was laughable.

The joking relationship between us had replaced the war, the feud between our two families, between our family names. The joking relationship between us succeeded in cleansing old insults with laughter and mockery.

But a totem is more serious. A totem is taboo. You can't eat it, you have to protect it. The Diops would risk their lives protecting a peacock in danger or a crowned crane about to die, because it's their totem. The Ndiayes don't need to protect lions from danger. A lion is never in danger. But it's said that lions never eat Ndiayes. The protection goes in both directions. I can't help but laugh when I think that the Diops are hardly in danger of being eaten by a peacock or a crowned crane. I can't help but smile when I think again of Mademba Diop laughing when I told him that the Diops weren't very smart for having chosen the peacock, or the crowned crane, as a totem. "The Diops are shortsighted egotists, like peacocks. They act proud, but their totem is just an arrogant fowl." This is what made Mademba laugh when I tried to make fun of him. Mademba simply replied that you don't choose your totem, it chooses you.

Unfortunately, I brought up his arrogant fowl totem again on the morning of his death, not long before Captain Armand whistled for the attack. And that's why he left before the others, why he shot out of the earth shrieking toward the enemy on the other side, to show us, me and the trench, that he was not a braggart, that he was brave. It's because of me that he left first. It's because of totems, because of our joking relationship and because of me, that Mademba Diop was disemboweled by a half-dead, blue-eyed enemy on that day.

VIII ₍ᵢᵢᵢ₎

ON THAT DAY, Mademba Diop wasn't thinking, despite all of his learning, all of his science. I know, I understand, I shouldn't have made fun of his totem. Until that day, I didn't think enough, I didn't reflect on half of what I said. You don't provoke your friend, your more-than-brother, to leave the belly of the earth screaming louder than anyone else. You don't drag your more-than-brother into temporary madness, into a place where a crowned crane couldn't last an instant, into a battlefield where not even the smallest plant can grow, not even the slightest shrub, as if thousands of locusts have been gorging themselves, without rest, month after month. A field sowed with thousands of tiny metallic seeds of war that produce no harvest. A scarred battlefield made for carnivores.

So here we are. Since I decided to think for myself, not to forbid myself any subject, I have come to understand that it wasn't the blue-eyed enemy from the other side who killed Mademba. It's me. I know, I understand why I didn't kill Mademba Diop when he begged me to. "You can't kill a man twice," a very, very quiet voice in my mind must have murmured to me. "You already killed your childhood friend," it must have whispered to me, "when you mocked his totem on a battle day and he leapt first from the belly of the earth. Wait a bit," my mind must have whispered in a very, very low voice, "wait a bit. Soon, when Mademba will be dead without your help, you'll understand. You'll understand that you didn't kill him, even though he asked you to, so as not to blame yourself for having finished the filthy job you began. Wait a bit," my mind must have whispered, "soon you will understand that you were Mademba Diop's blue-eyed enemy. You killed him with your words, you disemboweled him with your words, you devoured the insides of his body with your words."

From there to the thought that I am a dëmm, a devourer of souls, there's hardly any distance, any air. Since I've thought anything I want since then, I can admit everything to myself in the privacy of my mind. Yes, I told myself that I must be a dëmm, an eater of the insides of men. But I told myself, immediately after thinking it, that I couldn't believe such a thing, that it wasn't possible. At that time, it wasn't really me who was thinking. I had left the door of my mind open to the thoughts of others, which I mistook for my own. I wasn't hearing myself think anymore, but was hearing the others who were afraid of me. You have to be careful, when you believe you're free to think what you want, not to let in the thinking of others, in disguise, the false thinking of your father and mother, the spurious thinking of your grandfather, the masked thinking of your brother or sister, of your friends, in other words, of your enemies.

So I am not a dëmm, am not a devourer of souls. That's what the people who are afraid of me think. I am also not a savage. It's my Toubab sergeant and my blue-eyed enemies who think that. The thinking that is mine, the thinking that belongs to me, is that my mockery, my hurtful words about his totem, are the true cause of Mademba's death. It's because of my big mouth that he leapt shrieking from the belly of the earth to show me what I already knew, that he was brave. The question to answer is why I laughed at the totem of my more-than-brother. The question to answer is why my mind hatched words as sharp as a locust's bite on the day of an attack.

Because I loved Mademba, my more-than-brother. God's truth, I loved him so. I was so afraid he would die, I wanted so badly for the two of us to return safe and sound to Gandiol. I would have done anything to keep him alive. I followed him everywhere on the battlefield. As soon as Captain Armand would whistle for the attack so as to fully warn the enemy from the other side that we were about to come out shrieking from the belly of the earth, so as to warn the enemy to prepare to spray us with bullets, I would glue myself to Mademba so the bullet that hurt him would hurt me, or the bullet that killed him would kill me, or the bullet that missed him would miss me. God's truth, on attack days we were elbow to elbow on the battlefield, shoulder to shoulder. We ran shrieking toward the enemy on the other side in the same rhythm, we fired our guns at the same time, we were like twin brothers who come out the same day or the same night from their mother's womb.

And so, God's truth, I don't understand. No, I don't understand why one fine day I insinuated to Mademba Diop that he wasn't brave, that he wasn't a real warrior. To think for oneself doesn't necessarily mean to understand everything. God's truth, I don't understand why one fine day of bloody battle, without rhyme or reason, when I hoped we would return safe and sound, he and I, to Gandiol after the war, I killed Mademba Diop with my words. I do not understand at all.

IX III

AFTER THE SEVENTH SEVERED HAND, they'd had enough. They'd all had enough, the Toubab soldiers and the Chocolat soldiers. The sergeants and the not-sergeants. Captain Armand said that I must be tired, that I must rest. To tell me this, he called me to his dugout. It happened in the presence of a Chocolat, much older than me, higher ranked. A Chocolat with a Croix de Guerre and his heart in his boots, a Croix de Guerre Chocolat who translated whatever the captain wanted into Wolof. A poor old Croix de Guerre Chocolat who thought, as did the others, that I was a dëmm, a devourer of souls, and who trembled like a little leaf in the wind without daring to look at me, his left hand gripping a talisman in his pocket.

Like the others, he was afraid that I would devour the insides of his body, that I would bring him to his death. Like the others, white or black, the infantryman Ibrahima Seck trembled when our eyes met. That night, he prayed silently for a long time. That night, he fingered his worry beads for a long time to protect himself from me and from my contamination. That night, he purified himself. As he stood listening, the elder Ibrahima Seck was terrified to have to translate the captain's words for me. God's truth, he was terrified to inform me that I was being given exceptional permission to spend an entire month at the Rear! Because, in Ibrahima Seck's mind, what the captain ordered couldn't come as good news to me. Because my elder, the Croix de Guerre Chocolat, believed I wouldn't be happy to learn that I was being separated from my larder, from my prey, from my hunting ground. In Ibrahima Seck's mind, a sorcerer like me would certainly be very, very angry at the bearer of this bad news. God's truth, it would be no easy thing to escape a soldier sorcerer you've deprived of an entire month of prey, whom you've deprived of souls, friend or foe, to devour on the battlefield. In Ibrahima Seck's mind, I must be holding him responsible for the loss of all the insides of soldiers, friend or foe, I could have eaten. And so, to distance himself from my evil eye, to shield himself from the consequences of my anger, to be able to show his grandchildren, one day, his Croix de Guerre, the elder Ibrahima Seck began each of his sentences with the same words: "The captain says . . ."

"The captain says that you need to rest. The captain says that you are really very, very brave, but also very, very tired. The captain says that he salutes your courage, your very, very profound courage. The captain says that you are going to be given the Croix de Guerre like me . . . Ah! You already have one? . . . The captain says maybe you're going to get another one."

So yes, I know, I understand that Captain Armand no longer wanted me on the battlefield. Behind the words reported by the elder Croix de Guerre Chocolat Ibrahima Seck, I knew, I understood, that they'd had enough after the seven severed hands I brought home. Yes, I understood, God's truth, that on the battlefield they wanted only fleeting madness. Madmen of rage, madmen of pain, furious madmen, but temporary ones. No continuous madmen. As soon as the fighting ends, we're to file away our rage, our pain, and our fury. Pain is tolerated, we can bring our pain home on the condition that we keep it to ourselves. But rage and fury cannot be brought back to the trench. Before returning home, we must denude ourselves of rage and fury, we must strip ourselves of it, and if we don't we are no longer playing the game of war. Madness, after the captain blows the whistle to retreat, is taboo.

I knew, I understood that the captain and Ibrahima Seck, the Chocolat infantryman with the Croix de Guerre, didn't want any warrior's rage in our midst. God's truth, I understood that for them, with my seven severed hands, it was as if I had brought back screams and moans into a place of calm. It was impossible for them, seeing the severed hand of an enemy from the other side, to keep from thinking, And if it were mine? It was impossible for them to keep themselves from thinking, I've had enough of this war. God's truth, after battle we became human again for the enemy. We can't celebrate the fear of the enemy from the other side for long, when we ourselves are afraid. The severed hands are our fear, brought inside from outside the trench.

"The captain says that he thanks you again for your bravery. The captain says that you have been granted a month of leave. The captain says that he would like to know where you have . . . hidden, uh . . . put the severed hands."

And so, without hesitating, I heard myself reply:

"I no longer have the hands."

X III

GOD'S TRUTH, the captain and my elder Ibrahima Seck took me for an idiot. I may be a little strange, but I'm no idiot. I will never reveal where I hid my severed hands. They are my hands, I know which blue-eyes they belonged to. I know the provenance of each one. They had had blond or red hair on their backs, rarely black. Some were fleshy, others flaky. Their nails turned black after I separated them from their arms. One hand is smaller than the others, as if it were a woman's or a large child's. Little by little, they became stiff before rotting. So, to preserve them, after the second one, I slipped into the kitchen of the trench we called home, I sprinkled them very, very heavily with coarse salt, and I placed them in the cooling oven beneath the still-warm ash. I left them there for an entire night. In the morning, very, very early, I went to retrieve them. Then, the next day, I put them in the same place after having salted them again. And again and again, until they became like dried fish. I dried the hands of the blue-eyes the way at home we dry fish we want to preserve.

Now my seven hands—out of eight, I'm missing one thanks to Jean-Baptiste's pranks—now my seven hands have lost their individual characteristics. They're all the same, tanned and smoothed like camel leather, they have no more hair, blond or red or black. God's truth, they have no red spots or beauty marks. They're all a dark brown. Mummified. There's no chance their flesh will rot now. Nobody will be able to sniff them out, except the rats. They are in a safe place.

I thought how I had only seven because my friend Jean-Baptiste, the trickster, the joker, had stolen one, and I'd let him, because it was my first severed hand and it was beginning to rot. I didn't know yet what to do with it. I hadn't yet had the idea to dry them the way the fishermen's wives in Gandiol dry fish.

In Gandiol, we dry fish from the river or the sea in the

sun and with smoke after salting it very, very well. Here, there isn't any real sun. There's only a cold sun that doesn't dry anything. Mud remains mud. Blood never dries. Our uniforms only dry by the fire. That's why we make fires. Not only to try to warm ourselves. Mostly to dry ourselves.

But our fires in the trench are minuscule. Big fires are forbidden, the captain said. Because there is no smoke without fire, the captain said. As soon as they see smoke rising from our home, as soon as they notice the smallest thread of smoke, even from a cigarette, with their piercing blue eyes, the enemies on the other side will adjust their artillery and bombard us. Like us, the enemy on the other side bombards trenches at random. Like us, the enemy launches random salvos even on truce days, when there are no infantry attacks. So, best not to provide any targets to the enemy artillerymen. So, God's truth, best to avoid revealing our position with the blue smoke from a fire! So now our uniforms are never dry, so now our dirty uniforms and all of our clothes are always damp. So we try to make small fires without smoke. We position the kitchen stovepipe at the rear. So, God's truth, we try to be cleverer than our enemy with the piercing blue eyes. And so the kitchen stove was the only place where I could dry the hands. God's truth, I saved them all, even the second and the third, which were already half-gone.

At first, my trench-mates were so happy that I was bringing them enemy hands, they even touched them. From the first to the third, they dared to touch them. Some even spit on them, laughing. By the time I returned to the belly of the earth with my second enemy hand, my friend Jean-Baptiste had rifled through my things. He'd stolen my first hand, and I let him because it was beginning to spoil and to attract rats. I never liked the first hand, it wasn't pretty. It had long red hairs on its backside and I'd cut it off poorly, I had severed it roughly from the arm because I hadn't yet formed the habit. God's truth, my machete wasn't sharp enough yet. But then, with experience, by the fourth one I was able to separate the hand from an enemy arm in a single slice, in a single very clean cut with the blade of my machete that I spent hours sharpening before the captain would whistle for us to attack.

So, my friend Jean-Baptiste rifled through my things to steal the first enemy hand, which I didn't like. Jean-Baptiste was my only real white friend in the trench. He was the only Toubab who came to console me after the death of Mademba Diop. The others had touched my shoulder, the Chocolats had recited ritual prayers before they took Mademba's body to the Rear. The Chocolat soldiers didn't speak to me again about it because for them Mademba's was one death among the rest. They too had lost friends, more-than-brothers. They too wept inside for their dead. Only Jean-Baptiste had done more than place a hand on my shoulder when I brought Mademba Diop's disemboweled body back to the trench. Jean-Baptiste, with his round head and his clear blue eyes, had taken care of me. Jean-Baptiste, with his narrow waist and small hands, had helped me to wash my dirty clothes. Jean-Baptiste had given me tobacco. Jean-Baptiste had shared his bread with me. Jean-Baptiste had made me laugh.

And so, when Jean-Baptiste rifled through my things to steal my first enemy hand, I let him do it.

Jean-Baptiste had a lot of fun with that severed hand. Jean-Baptiste laughed a lot with the enemy hand that had begun to rot. From the first morning when he stole it, from that first breakfast, he shook all of our hands with that hand, one after the other. And when he saluted any of us, we knew, we understood, that he was extending the severed hand of the enemy instead of his own, which was hidden beneath the sleeve of his uniform.

It was Albert who got stuck with the enemy hand. Albert screamed when he realized that Jean-Baptiste had left the enemy hand behind in his. Albert screamed even as he threw the enemy hand on the ground and everyone laughed and everyone made fun of him, even noncommissioned officers, and even the captain, God's truth. So Jean-Baptiste cried out, "Bunch of idiots! Every one of you has shaken the hand of the enemy, you will all be court-martialed!" So everyone laughed again, even the elder Croix de Guerre Chocolat Ibrahima Seck, who translated for us what Jean-Baptiste had said.

XI ...

BUT, GOD'S TRUTH, that first severed hand brought no luck to Jean-Baptiste. Jean-Baptiste didn't stay my friend for long. Not because we stopped liking each other but because Jean-Baptiste died. He died a very, very ugly death. He died with my enemy hand attached to his helmet. Jean-Baptiste liked to joke, to play the idiot, too much. There are limits, it isn't good to play with the hands of the blue-eyed enemy in front of enemies with blue eyes doubled by binoculars. Jean-Baptiste shouldn't have provoked them, he shouldn't have made fun of them. The enemies from the other side resented him. They didn't like seeing their friend's hand stuck to the point of a Rosalie bayonet. They were sick and tired of watching it wave in the sky above our trench. God's truth, they'd had enough of Jean-Baptiste's antics, like when he would cry out, at the top of his lungs, with their friend's hand on the end of his bayonet, "Filthy Krauts! Filthy Krauts!" It was as if Jean-Baptiste had gone mad, and I knew, I understood why.

Jean-Baptiste had become a provocateur. Jean-Baptiste had been trying to draw the attention of the blue-eyed enemies behind their binoculars ever since he received a certain perfumed letter. I knew, I understood, when I saw his face as he read that letter. Jean-Baptiste's face was alive with laughter and light before he opened the perfumed letter. When he finished reading the perfumed letter, Jean-Baptiste's face had become gray. No more light. Only the laugh remained. But his laugh was no longer a laugh of happiness. His laugh had become the laugh of misery. A laugh that was like tears, an unpleasant laugh, a false laugh. After the perfumed letter, Jean-Baptiste helped himself to my first enemy hand so he could make crude gestures at the enemies on the other side. Jean-Baptiste made asses of them by waving it in the sky above our trench, stuck on the end of his rifle's Rosalie: the enemy hand whose middle finger he had raised. He'd yell, "Up your ass, Krauts, go fuck yourselves!" shaking his rifle so that the enemy's matching blue eyes would be sure to receive his message, so that there was no way his middle finger would go unnoticed.

Captain Armand told him to stop. To act out like Jean-Baptiste wasn't good for anyone. Jean-Baptiste might as well be setting fires inside the trench. His insults had the power of smoke. The power to help the enemy from the other side adjust their aim. It was as if he had given himself over to the enemy. There was no point in dying if it wasn't at the captain's command. God's truth, I knew, I understood, as did the captain and the others, that Jean-Baptiste wanted to die, to torment the blue-eyed enemies and become their target.

So, one morning after our captain whistled for the attack, when we leapt shrieking from the belly of the earth, the blue-eyed enemies didn't fire immediately. The blue-eyed enemies waited twenty breaths before firing on us, the time it took to identify Jean-Baptiste. God's truth, to identify him, at least twenty breaths. I know, I understood, we all understood why they waited before firing on us. The blue-eyed enemies, the captain said, held a grudge against Jean-Baptiste. God's truth, they'd had enough of hearing him shout "Up yours, Krauts!" with their friend's hand stuck to the end of a Rosalie bayonet, waving in the sky above our trench. The enemies on the other side were intent on killing

Jean-Baptiste the next time the French attacked. They said to themselves, "We're going to kill that one in a particularly disgusting way, to set an example."

And that idiot Jean-Baptiste, who'd made it clear that he wanted to die at any cost, did all he could to facilitate the task. He attached the enemy hand to the front of his helmet. And as it continued to rot, he wrapped it in gauze—he "turbaned" it, as the captain said—in white gauze, one finger at a time. And Jean-Baptiste did a very good job because you could see it very clearly, the hand attached to the front of his helmet, its middle finger up in the air, the others folded down. The enemies with matching blue eyes didn't have a hard time identifying him. They had binoculars. In their binoculars they saw a white spot on the top of a slender soldier's helmet. That must have taken five breaths. They adjusted their binoculars and they saw that the small white spot was giving them the finger. Five more halting breaths. But to perfect their aim must have taken longer, ten slow breaths at least, because they were so angry at Jean-Baptiste for mocking them with their friend's hand. But they were ready. And as soon as they saw him in their cannon's scope, twenty breaths after our captain's whistle, they must have been happy, the enemies on the other side. And they must have been very, very happy when, through their binoculars, they saw Jean-Baptiste's head fly off. His head, his helmet, and the enemy hand he had attached to it: pulverized. That must have made them so happy, the enemies with their matching blue eyes, to see their dishonor pulverized along with the culprit's head. God's truth, they must have offered tobacco to whoever pulled off such a beautiful feat. As soon as our attack was over, they must have slapped him on the shoulder, passed him a drink. They must have applauded him for his perfect shot. They might even have written a song in his honor.

God's truth, it might have been this song in his honor that I heard rise from their trench, the evening of the attack in which Jean-Baptiste died, the evening when for the fourth time I severed the hand of an enemy from the other side, after placing the insides of his body outside, in the heart of la terre à personne, "no-man's-land," as the captain said.

XII _{III}

I HEARD THE SINGING OF THE ENEMIES with matching blue eyes very clearly, because that evening I happened to be right next to their trench. God's truth, I had crawled right up to them without their seeing me, and I waited until they'd finished singing before I caught one. I waited until silence fell, until they had relaxed, and I extracted one like you'd extract a tiny baby from its mother's belly, with a violent tenderness to minimize the shock, to minimize the sound. I did it this way because I wanted to catch the master artilleryman who had killed Jean-Baptiste. That evening, God's truth, I took many risks to avenge my friend Jean-Baptiste, who had wanted to die because of a perfumed letter.

I crawled for hours beneath the barbed wire to get right next to their trench. I covered myself in mud so they wouldn't see me. Immediately after the shell that decapitated Jean-Baptiste, I threw myself on the ground and crawled for hours in the mud. Captain Armand had long since whistled for the attack to end when I arrived right next to the enemy trench, which was also open like the sex of an enormous woman, a woman the size of the earth. So I moved even closer to the edge of the enemy's domain and then I waited, waited. For a long time they sang the songs of men, the songs of soldiers, beneath the stars. I waited, waited until they fell asleep. Except one. Except one who'd leaned up against the wall of the trench to smoke. You shouldn't smoke in a war, the enemy will spot you. I spotted him because of his tobacco smoke, thanks to the blue smoke that rose into the sky from his trench.

God's truth, I took an enormous risk. As soon as I noticed, a few steps to my left, the blue smoke rising into the black sky, I slid like a snake along the side of the trench. I was covered with mud from head to toe. I was like the mamba snake that takes on the color of the earth on which it slithers. I was invisible and I slid, slid, slid as fast as I could to get myself right next to the blue smoke the enemy soldier was blowing into the black air. I really took a big risk and that's why what I did that night, for my white friend who wanted to die at war, I did only once.

Without knowing what was happening in the trench, without being able to see a thing, I slung my head and my arms into the enemy trench. I blindly dangled the top half of my body into the trench to capture the blue-eyed enemy who was smoking below me. God's truth, I was lucky the trench had no roof in that spot. I was lucky the enemy soldier who was blowing blue smoke into the black sky was alone. I was lucky to be able to clap my hand over his mouth before he had a chance to scream. God's truth, I lucked out that the proprietor of my fourth trophy was small and light, like a child of fifteen or sixteen. In my collection of hands, he gave me the smallest one. I was lucky that night not to be spotted by the friends, by the trench-mates of the little blue-eyed soldier. They must all have been sleeping, worn out by the day's attack, in which Jean-Baptiste was killed first by the master artilleryman. After Jean-Baptiste's head fell, they had continued to fire, enraged, without stopping to breathe. Many of my trench-mates died on that day. But I managed to run, to fire, to throw myself on my belly and crawl beneath the barbed wire. Firing as I ran, throwing myself on my belly and crawling into la terre à personne, "no-man's-land," as the captain said.

God's truth, the enemies on the other side were very tired. That night, they lowered their guard after singing. I don't know why the little enemy soldier wasn't tired that night. Why he went to smoke his tobacco after his trench-mates had gone to sleep. God's truth, it was fate that made me capture him and not someone else. It was written on high that it would be him I would find in the middle of the night in the hot pit of the enemy trench. Now I know, I understand that nothing is simple about what's written on high. I know, I understand, but I don't tell anyone because now I think what I want, for no one but myself, ever since Mademba Diop died. I believe I understand that what's written on high is only a copy of what man writes here below. God's truth, I believe that God always lags behind us. It's all He can do to assess the damage. He couldn't have wanted me to catch the little blue-eyed soldier in the hot pit of the enemy trench.

I don't believe the proprietor of the fourth hand in my collection had done anything wrong. I could read it in his blue eyes when I gutted him in la terre à personne, "no-man's-land," as the captain said. I could see in his eyes that he was a good boy, a good son, still too young to have known a woman, but a good future husband, certainly. And here I had to fall on him, like death and destruction on innocence. That's war: it's when God lags behind the music of men, when he can't untangle the threads of so many fates at the same time. God's truth, you can't blame God. Who's to say He didn't want to punish the parents of the little enemy soldier by making him die at war by my black hand? Who's to say He didn't want to punish the little enemy soldier's grandparents because He'd run out of time to redress the suffering they'd caused their own children? Who's to say? God's truth, God may have lagged behind in his punishment of the little enemy soldier's family. I am well positioned to know that he did punish them, gravely, by punishing their son or grandson. Because the little enemy soldier suffered as did the others when I extracted the insides of his body to expose them to the air outside, in a little pile next to his still-living body. But I really did come to pity him, very, very quickly. I minimized the punishment, through him, of his grandparents or parents. I let him beg me only once, tears in eyes, before I finished him off. He could not have been the one who disemboweled my more-than-brother Mademba Diop. He also could not have been the one who pulverized, with a single shell, the head of my friend Jean-Baptiste, the joker driven to despair by a perfumed letter.

And maybe the little blue-eyed enemy soldier was standing guard when I threw myself headfirst into the hot trench, arms outstretched, without knowing who I would catch. I carried him out with his gun hitched to his shoulder. A soldier standing guard shouldn't smoke. Any blue smoke, in the darkest night, is visible. That's how I spotted him, my little blue-eyed soldier, proprietor of my fourth trophy, of my fourth hand. But, God's truth, I pitied him in no-man's-land. I killed him as soon as he begged me, once, with his blue eyes filled with tears. It was God who'd made him stand guard.

It was after I returned to the trench that was our home with my fourth small hand and the gun it had cleaned, oiled, loaded, and fired that my soldier-friends, white and black, avoided me like the plague. When I returned home crawling in the mud like a black mamba returning to its nest after rat-hunting, no one dared touch me anymore. No one was happy to see me. They must have believed that the first hand brought bad luck to that little fool Jean-Baptiste and that the evil eye would fall on anyone who touched me or even looked at me. And Jean-Baptiste wasn't there anymore to rally the others to rejoice at seeing me return alive. Everything is double: one side good, one bad. Jean-Baptiste, when he was still alive, showed the others the good side of my trophies: "Look, here's our pal Alfa with another hand and the rifle that goes with it. Let's celebrate, friends! This means fewer Kraut bullets aimed at us! Fewer Kraut hands, fewer Kraut bullets. Glory to Alfa!" That's how the rest of the soldiers, black or white, Chocolat or Toubab, were rallied to congratulate me for having brought back my trophies to our dark trench, open to the sky. They all applauded me up to the third hand. I was courageous, I was a force of nature, like the captain said many times. God's truth, they gave me good things to eat, they helped me clean up; above all Jean-Baptiste, who liked me. But on the night Jean-Baptiste died, when I returned to our trench the way a mamba slithers back into its nest after the hunt, they avoided me like the plague. The bad side of my crimes had won out over the good side. The Chocolat soldiers began to whisper that I was a soldier sorcerer, a dëmm, a devourer of souls, and the white Toubab soldiers were starting to believe them. God's truth, each thing carries its opposite within. Up to the third hand, I was a war hero, beginning with the fourth I became a dangerous madman, a bloodthirsty savage. God's truth, that's how things go, that's how the world is: each thing is double.

XIII _{III}

THEY THOUGHT I WAS AN IDIOT, but I'm not. The captain and the old Chocolat Croix de Guerre infantryman Ibrahima Seck wanted my seven hands so they could trap me. God's truth, they wanted proof of my savagery so they could lock me up, but I would never tell them where I'd hidden my seven hands. They would never find them. They couldn't imagine the quiet spot where they'd been laid to rest, dried and wrapped in cloth. God's truth, without these seven pieces of proof, they would have no choice but to send me temporarily to the Rear to rest. God's truth, they would have no choice but to hope that upon my return from the Rear the soldiers with matching blue eyes would kill me so they would be rid of me without too much bother. In war, when you have a problem with one of your soldiers, you get the enemy to kill him. It's more practical.

Between my fifth hand and my sixth hand, the Toubab soldiers stopped wanting to obey Captain Armand when he whistled for the attack. One fine day they said, "No! We've had enough!" They even said to Captain Armand, "You may as well be whistling for the attack so the enemy on the other side will be ready to gun us down as soon as we leave the trench. We won't leave it anymore. We refuse to die for your whistle!" And then the captain replied, "What, just like that, you won't obey orders?" The Toubab soldiers replied immediately, "No, we don't want to obey your whistle of death!" When the captain was very sure that they wouldn't obey anymore, and when he saw that it was now only seven of them and not the fifty it had been at the start, he made the seven culprits stand in the middle of the rest of us and commanded, "Tie their hands behind their backs!" Once they had their hands tied behind their backs, the captain yelled at them, "You are cowards, you are the shame of France! You are afraid to die for your fatherland, and yet you are going to die today!"

What the captain made us do then is very, very ugly. God's truth, we never would have believed that we'd be treating our fellow soldiers like enemies from the other side. The captain told us to hold our loaded rifles to their jaws and to kill them if they didn't obey his final order. We were on one side of the trench, where it was open to the skies of war, and our traitorous friends were on the other, a few paces from us. Our traitorous friends turned their backs to us, so they were facing the little ladders. Seven little ladders. The little ladders we climbed to rise out of the trench when we would launch an assault on the enemy from the other side. So, once everyone was in their place, the captain shouted at them, "You have betrayed France! But those who obey my final order will be given a posthumous Croix de Guerre. For the rest of you, we'll write to your families that you are deserters, traitors who sold out to the enemy. For traitors, there is no military pension. Nothing for your wives, nothing for your families!" Then the captain whistled for the attack so that our friends would climb out of our trench and be gunned down by the enemy from the other side.

God's truth, I've never seen anything so ugly. Even before the captain whistled for the attack, some of our seven traitorous friends clattered their teeth, others pissed their pants. As soon as the captain whistled, it was terrible. If the moment weren't so dire, you could almost have laughed. Because with their hands tied behind their backs, our traitorous friends had a hard time climbing the six or seven stairs of the attack ladders. They stumbled, they slid, they fell on their knees and screamed in fear because the enemies with matching blue eyes understood almost at once that our captain was delivering them their prey. God's truth, as soon as the master artilleryman who had killed my friend Jean-Baptiste saw the gift he was being offered, he launched three small malicious shells that all missed their intended target. But the fourth one exploded on one of our traitorous friends who had just emerged from the trench, a traitorous friend who was being brave for his wife and children, whose insides flew out of his body to splatter us with black blood. God's truth, though I was already used to it, my white and black fellow soldiers were not. And we cried a lot, especially our traitorous friends who were condemned to climb out from the trench to be massacred one by one, or else no Croix de Guerre, the captain had said. No pension for their parents, no pension for their wives or for their children.

God's truth, the leader of the traitorous friends was brave. The leader of our traitorous friends was named Alphonse. God's truth, Alphonse was a real warrior. A real warrior is not afraid to die. Alphonse climbed out of our trench stumbling like an invalid and crying, "Now I know why I must die! I know why. I am dying for your pension, Odette! I love you, Odette! I love you, Ode . . ." And then a fifth small malicious shell decapitated him just like Jean-Baptiste, because the master artilleryman from the other side had begun to hit his marks. His brains rained on us and on the other traitorous friends who screamed with terror because they had to die like their traitorous leader, Alphonse. God's truth, we all wept at the death of the leader of our traitorous friends. The elder Chocolat Croix de Guerre infantryman Ibrahima Seck translated what Alphonse had cried out. Odette was lucky to have had him as a husband. That Alphonse was really somebody.

But after Alphonse, there were five left. Five more had to die after the leader of our traitorous friends. One of them turned toward us, weeping and crying out, "Have pity! Have pity! Guys . . . guys . . . pity . . ." This traitorous friend was Albert, who couldn't care less about the Croix de Guerre, about the captain's posthumous pensions. This one didn't think about his parents, his wife, his children. Maybe he didn't have any. The captain yelled "Fire!" and we fired. There were four left. Four temporarily surviving traitorous friends. These four traitorous friends were brave for their families. These four traitorous friends leapt one by one from the trench, flailing like chickens who have just been decapitated and keep running for a while. But the master artilleryman from the other side seemed, for the duration of about thirty breaths, to be done with wasting those little shells. He seemed to be waiting, for about thirty breaths, while looking through his binoculars at the sacrifices we were sending.

He had already downed two, after three missed shots. Five small shells, that was enough. In war, you can't waste heavy munitions just to impress the enemy, as the captain said. So the last four traitorous friends had to die by vulgar machine-gun fire, all together, their final screams stuck in their throats.

God's truth, after the deaths of the seven traitorous friends commanded by the captain, there was no more revolt. No more rebellion. God's truth, I know, I understand that if the captain had wanted to have me killed by the enemies from the other side, the minute I returned from the Rear, he would have succeeded. I know, I understand that if he wanted me dead he would have gotten what he wanted.

But I could not let the captain know what I knew. God's truth, I couldn't reveal the location of the severed hands. So I responded to the captain who asked me in the voice of the elder Croix de Guerre Chocolat Ibrahima Seck where the severed hands of the enemy from the other side had gone that I didn't know, that I had lost them, that maybe one of the traitorous friends had stolen them to cast suspicion on the rest of us. "Fine, fine," replied the captain, "let the hands stay where they are. Let them stay invisible. It's all right, all right . . . But still, you must be tired. Your way of waging war is a little too savage. I never ordered you to cut off enemy hands! It isn't regulation. But I looked the other way because of your Croix de Guerre. You understand, fundamentally, what it means for a Chocolat to put himself in the line of fire. Go rest for a month at the Rear and return refreshed and ready for combat. But you have to promise me that when you get back you'll stop mutilating the enemy, understood? You will content yourself with killing them, not mutilating them. The civilities of war forbid it. Understood? You leave tomorrow."

I would have understood nothing of what the captain said to me if Ibrahima Seck, the elder Croix de Guerre Chocolat, hadn't translated it for me, beginning all of his sentences with "Captain Armand says that . . ." But I counted close to twenty breaths during the captain's speech and only twelve in the speech of my elder Ibrahima Seck. There was, then, something in the captain's speech that the Croix de Guerre Chocolat did not translate.

Captain Armand is a small man with matching black eyes drowning in continuous rage. His matching black eyes are full of hate for anything that isn't war. For the captain, life is war. The captain loves war the way men love a capricious woman. The captain indulges war shamelessly. He showers war with presents, he spoils her with countless soldiers' lives. The captain is a devourer of souls. I know, I understand that Captain Armand was a dëmm who needed his wife, war, to survive, just the way she needed a husband like him to support her.

I know, I understand that Captain Armand would do

whatever possible to continue to make love to war. I understand that he saw me as a dangerous rival who could spoil his whole love affair with war. God's truth, the captain wanted to be rid of me. I knew, I understood that when I returned I might be given a non-combat job somewhere else. God's truth, I knew that I had to retrieve my hands from where I'd hidden them. But I also knew, I also understood that that was what the captain was hoping for. He would have me surveilled, maybe even by the elder Croix de Guerre Chocolat Ibrahima Seck. God's truth, he wanted my seven hands, to use them as evidence and have me shot, to use them as cover, so he could continue to make love to war. He would have someone rifle through my bags before I left. As Jean-Baptiste said, he would like to catch me red-handed. But I'm no idiot. God's truth, I knew, I understood what I had to do.

XIV ₪

I'M DOING WELL, I'm at ease in the Rear. In this place, I do almost nothing for myself anymore. I sleep, I eat, beautiful young women dressed in white take care of me, and that's it. No noise from explosions, from machine-gun fire, from small murderous shells launched by the enemy from the other side.

I didn't come alone to this place in the Rear. I came with my seven enemy hands. And I took them from right under the captain's nose. Under his nose, as Jean-Baptiste used to say. God's truth, they were barely hidden, there in the bottom of my soldier's trunk. Despite their being swaddled in the strips of white cloth with which I'd carefully wrapped them, I recognized each one. My trench-mates, black and white soldiers who had received orders from the captain to rifle through my things before I left, didn't dare open my trunk. God's truth, they were afraid. I helped them be afraid. In place of my padlock, attached by a string to the trunk's handle, I had hung a talisman. God's truth, a handsome talisman made of red leather that my father, the old man, gave me when I left for the war. On this handsome talisman made of red leather I had drawn something that caused any spies, black or white, Chocolat or Toubab, to drop my things and run. I really worked hard on the drawing, God's truth, I made an effort. I drew on the red leather talisman with a small very pointy rat bone dipped in ash mixed with lamp oil, I drew a small black hand cut off at the wrist. Such a small hand, really tiny, with its five little fingers spread out, swollen at the base, like the fingers of that translucent pink lizard we call an Ounk. The Ounk has skin so delicate and pink that, even at dusk, you can see the insides of its body, its guts. The Ounk is dangerous, it pees poison.

God's truth, the hand that I drew was effective. Once the talisman was attached to the handle of my trunk, all the men who had been ordered by the captain to open it and look for my seven hands, which I had no need to hide elsewhere, must have lied to him. They must have sworn to him that they searched for the seven hands in vain. But what's certain is that, white or black, they hadn't dared to touch my trunk that was locked with a talisman. How would the same soldiers who couldn't dare look at me after my fourth hand be able to open my trunk, locked with a bloodred talisman, a talisman tattooed with the image of a little black severed hand, its fingers swollen at the base like an Ounk's? In that moment I was happy to pass for a dëmm, a devourer of souls. When the elder Croix de Guerre Chocolat Ibrahima Seck came to inspect my things, he must have nearly fainted at the sight of my mystical padlock. He must have reproached himself for laying eyes on it at all. Anyone who saw my mystical padlock, God's truth, must have reproached himself for being too curious. When I think about all those curious cowards, I can't help but laugh very, very loudly in my head.

I don't laugh in front of people the way I laugh in my head. My old father always said to me, "Only children and fools laugh without reason." I am no longer a child. God's truth, war made me grow up all at once, especially after the death of my more-than-brother Mademba Diop. But despite his death, I still laugh. Despite the death of Jean-Baptiste, I still laugh in my head. For others I just smile, I only allow myself a smile. God's truth, smiles inspire smiles, just like yawns. I smile at people, they smile back. They can't hear, when I smile at them, the thundering laughter resounding in my head. Which is lucky, because they'd take me for a lunatic otherwise. It's the same with the severed hands. They didn't divulge what I had forced their bearers to suffer, they didn't show anyone those steaming entrails in the cold of la terre à personne, as the captain said. The severed hands didn't show how I eviscerated eight blue-eyed enemies. God's truth, no one asked me any questions about how I got my hands. Not even Jean-Baptiste, dead by decapitation from a small malicious shell launched by a master artilleryman with matching blue eyes. The seven hands that I have left are like my smile, they show and hide simultaneously the destomaching of enemies that makes me explode with secret laughter.

Laughter brings laughter and smiles bring smiles. Because I smile at everyone in the recuperation center at the Rear, everyone smiles at me. God's truth, even my fellow soldiers, Chocolat and Toubab, who scream in the middle of the night when they hear the attack whistle and the endless noise of war in their heads, even they, as soon as they see me smile, smile back. They can't help themselves, God's truth, it's beyond their control.

Doctor François, who is a tall thin man with a sad expression, also smiled at me when I first appeared before him. Whereas the captain told me that I was a force of nature, Doctor François told me with his eyes that I have a nice face. God's truth, Doctor François likes me. While he withholds his smile in front of the others, he shares it with me freely. All this because smiles inspire smiles.

But, God's truth, of all the smiles that I've purchased with my own perpetual smile, my favorite is that of Mademoiselle François, one of the numerous women dressed in nurses' whites. God's truth, Mademoiselle François likes me a lot. God's truth, Mademoiselle François agrees with her father without knowing it. She's also said to me with her eyes that I have a nice face. But then she looked at the middle of my body in a way that made me understand she was thinking about something more than just my face. I knew, I understood, I guessed that she wanted to make love to me. I knew, I understood, I guessed that she wanted to see me naked. I saw it in the way she looked at me, just like Fary Thiam, who had let me take her in a small forest of ebony trees not far from the river, a few hours before I left for the war.

FARY THIAM HAD taken me by the hand, looked me in the eyes, and then, discreetly, farther down. Then Fary had separated herself from the circle of friends we were with. And, a little after she left, I said goodbye to everyone else and I followed Fary, at a distance, as she headed toward the river. In Gandiol, people don't like to walk at night near the shores of the river because of the goddess Mame Coumba Bang. Fary Thiam and I didn't see anyone, thanks to this fear of the river goddess. Fary and I were too, too eager to make love to be afraid.

God's truth, Fary didn't look back a single time. She was headed toward a little forest of ebony trees not far from the river below. She disappeared into it and I followed her. When I found her, I saw that Fary had her back up against a tree. She was standing facing me, she was waiting for me. It was a full moon, but the ebony trees were so close together they shaded out the moon. I saw Fary with her back up against a tree, but God's truth, I couldn't even see her face. Fary pulled me against her and I could tell that she was naked. Fary Thiam smelled like incense and the green waters of the river. Fary undressed me and I let her do it. Fary pulled me down to the ground and I lay on top of her. Before Fary, I had never known a woman, before me Fary had not known a man. Without knowing how to do it, I entered the interior of the middle of Fary's body. God's truth, the interior of Fary's body was incredibly soft, warm, and wet. I stayed there a long time without moving, palpating in Fary's interior. Then all of a sudden she started to roll her hips against me, first gently and then more quickly. If I hadn't been inside Fary's insides, I would certainly have laughed because we must have been funny to see, because I too started to shake my pelvis in all directions, and each of my thrusts was returned by a thrust from Fary Thiam's pelvis. Fary thrust against me, moaning, and I returned her thrusts, moaning too. God's truth, if it hadn't been so good, if I'd taken the time to look at us wriggling against each other like that, I would have laughed a lot. But I couldn't laugh, I could only moan with joy when I was inside Fary Thiam's insides. After wriggling the middles of our bodies in all directions like that, what always happens happened that time too. I came inside Fary's insides and I cried out as I came. It was loud and much more beautiful than it was with my hand. Fary Thiam also cried out at the end. Happily nobody heard us.

When Fary and I got up, we could barely stand. I couldn't see her eyes in the dusk of the thicket of ebony trees. And yet the moon was full, it was enormous, it was almost yellow like a small sun reflected in the green river water. It extinguished the stars around it but the ebony trees protected us from its glow. Fary Thiam got dressed and helped me get dressed as she would a child. Fary kissed me on the cheek and then she went off in the direction of Gandiol without looking back. God's truth, I stayed there looking at the moon, ablaze on the river. I stayed there a long time watching the river on fire, not thinking about anything. God's truth, that was the last time I saw Fary Thiam before leaving for the war.

XV_{III}

MADEMOISELLE FRANÇOIS, one of Doctor François's numerous daughters dressed all in white, looked at me the way Fary Thiam had looked at me the night when she wanted us to make love beside the river on fire. I smiled at Mademoiselle François, who was a very beautiful young woman, like Fary. Mademoiselle François had matching blue eyes. Mademoiselle François returned my smile right away and her gaze lingered on the middle of my body. Mademoiselle François wasn't like her father, the doctor: God's truth, she is full of life. Mademoiselle François said to me with her matching blue eyes that she found me very handsome from top to bottom.

But if Mademba Diop, my more-than-brother, were still alive he would have said, "No, you're lying, she didn't say you're handsome. Mademoiselle François didn't say that she wanted you! You're lying, it's not true, you don't know how to speak French." But I didn't need to speak French to understand the language of Mademoiselle François's eyes. God's truth, I know I'm handsome, everyone's eyes tell me so. Blue eyes and black ones, women's eyes and men's. Fary Thiam's eyes told me so, as did those of all the women of Gandiol, whatever their age. The eyes of my friends, girls and boys, always said it when I was near-naked on the sand during a wrestling match. Even the eyes of Mademba Diop, my more-than-brother, that weakling, that scrawny thing, couldn't help but tell me during a wrestling match that I was the most handsome.

Mademba Diop had the right to tell me anything he wanted, to make fun of me, because the rules of joking relationships made it permissible. Mademba Diop could be ironic, could tease me about how I was, because he was my more-than-brother. But God's truth, Mademba could never say anything about my physique. I'm so handsome that, when I smile, everyone—except those men who have been sacrificed to no-man's-land—smiles back. When I show my teeth, which are very, very white and well aligned, even Mademba Diop, the biggest scoffer the earth has known, couldn't help but show his own foul teeth. But, God's truth, Mademba would never admit that he envied me my beautiful and very, very white teeth, my chest and my very, very broad shoulders, my waist and my flat stomach, my very muscular thighs. Mademba was happy to let his eyes tell me that he envied me and loved me at the same time. When I had won four wrestling matches in a row, glistening in the moonlight, a hostage to my admirers, Mademba's eyes always said: "I envy you, but I love you too." His eyes said: "I would love to be you, but I am proud of you." Like all things in this base world, the look Mademba gave me was double.

Now that I am far from the battle in which I lost my more-than-brother Mademba, far from the little malicious decapitating shells and the big red seeds of war falling from the metallic sky, far from Captain Armand and his whistle of death, far from my elder Croix de Guerre Chocolat Ibrahima Seck, I tell myself that I should never have made fun of my friend. Mademba had foul teeth, but he was brave. Mademba had the rib cage of a runt, but he was brave. Mademba had absurdly narrow hips, but he was a real warrior. I know, I understand that I should not have pushed him with my words to demonstrate a kind of courage I knew he already possessed. I know, I understand that it was because Mademba envied me and loved me at the same time that he went out first, as soon as Captain Armand blew the attack whistle on the day of his death. It was to show me that you don't need beautiful teeth, you don't need beautiful shoulders and a broad torso and very, very strong arms and thighs to be truly brave. So in the end I think it wasn't just my words that killed Mademba. It wasn't just my words about the Diops' totem, as hurtful as those grains of metal that fell on us from the sky of war, that killed him. I know, I understand that all of my beauty and all of my strength also killed Mademba, my more-than-brother, who loved me and envied me at the same time. It was the beauty and strength of my body that killed him, it was the way all the women looked at me, at the middle of my body, that killed him. It was the way their eyes caressed my shoulders, my chest, my arms, and my legs, the way they lingered on my well-aligned teeth and my proud, hooked nose that killed him.

Even before the war started, even before we left, Mademba Diop and I together, for the war, people tried to divide us. God's truth, the bad people of Gandiol had decided to separate us already by telling Mademba that I was a dëmm, that I was consuming his power and vitality little by little in his sleep. These people of Gandiol said to Mademba—I heard this from the mouth of Fary Thiam, whom we both loved—they said, "You see how Alfa Ndiaye is blooming with beauty and how you are skinny and ugly. It's because he's absorbing all of your power and vitality to your loss and his gain, for he is a dëmm, a devourer of souls who has no pity for you. Drop him, abandon him, or you'll be heading straight for your own dissolution. The insides of your body will dry up into dust!" But Mademba, despite these terrible words, never abandoned me, never left me alone with my resplendent beauty. God's truth, Mademba never believed I was a dëmm. To the contrary, when I saw Mademba come home with a busted lip, I believed that he'd been fighting to defend me against the bad people of Gandiol. It was Fary Thiam who told me this, just before we left, Mademba and I, for the war in France. It's thanks to Fary whom we both loved that I understood that despite his chest being narrow as a pigeon's, his arms and thighs being scarily thin, Mademba, my more-than-brother, didn't fear the punches of young men who were stronger than he was. God's truth, it's easier to be brave when you have a broad chest and arms, and thighs as thick and strong as mine. But the truly brave like Mademba are the ones who aren't afraid of punches even though they're weak. God's truth, now I can admit it to myself, Mademba was braver than me. But I know, I have understood too late that I should have said this to him before he died.

SO EVEN THOUGH I don't speak Mademoiselle François's French, I understood the language of her eyes on the middle of my body. It wasn't difficult to understand. It was the same as with Fary Thiam and all the other women who have wanted me.

But, God's truth, in the world before, I would never have wanted anyone other than Fary Thiam. Fary wasn't the most beautiful girl in my age set, but she was the one whose smile most moved me. Fary was very, very moving. Her voice was soft, like the lapping of the river against fishermen's canoes on quiet mornings. Fary's smile was the dawn, her ass round as dunes in the Lompoul desert. Fary had eyes that were both doe and lioness. At times an earth-shattering tornado, at others an ocean of tranquility. God's truth, I would have lost Mademba's friendship to win Fary's love. Luckily, Fary chose me over Mademba. Luckily, my more-than-brother deferred to me. It was because Fary chose me in front of everyone that Mademba stepped aside.

She chose me one night in deep winter. Among my age set we had planned an all-nighter, a vigil, a night without sleep to be spent dazzling one another with clever talk until dawn at Mademba's parents' place. We would drink Moorish tea and eat sweets with the girls in our age set in Mademba's compound. We would speak of love in surreptitious terms. We pooled our money and bought three packs of Moorish tea and a large cone of sugar wrapped in blue paper at the village store. With the sugar we made a hundred small millet cakes. We spread out wide mats on the fine sand of Mademba's compound. When night fell, we set seven small red-enamel teapots on the glowing iron cradles of seven small coal fires crackling with sparks. We had carefully displayed the small millet cakes on large metal platters, imitation French faïence borrowed from the village store. We had put on our most handsome shirts, the lightest ones possible so we would be resplendent in the moonlight. I did not have a button-up shirt. Mademba lent me one that was too small for me, but I was resplendent anyway when the eighteen young girls of our age set made their entrance into Mademba's family's place.

We had lived sixteen years and we all wanted Fary Thiam, though she wasn't the most beautiful. And Fary Thiam chose me from among everyone. As soon as she saw me sitting on the mat, she came to sit cross-legged next to me; God's truth, right next to me, so that my right thigh and her left thigh touched. God's truth, I thought my heart would break my ribs from the inside, the way it beat, beat, beat. God's truth, from that moment I knew what it meant to be happy. There is no joy greater than the joy Fary caused when she chose me beneath the shining light of the moon.

We had lived sixteen years and we wanted to laugh. We took turns telling short funny stories full of double entendres, we invented guessing games. Mademba's little brothers and sisters, who had been asleep, heard us and came to join us, one by one. And I felt like the king of the world because Fary had chosen me and not anyone else. I took Fary's left hand and pressed it in my right hand and she let me have it, confident. God's truth, Fary Thiam has no equal. But Fary didn't want to give herself to me. Each time I asked her to let me enter the insides of her body after that night when she chose me over everyone in my age set, she refused. Fary always said "no," "no," and "no," for four years. A boy and a girl from the same age set do not make love. Even if they've chosen each other as intimate friends for life, a boy and a girl of the same age set must never become husband and wife. I knew this, I was aware of this peasant law. God's truth, I knew this ancestral rule, but I did not accept it.

Maybe I began to think for myself long before Mademba's death. As the captain liked to say, there's no smoke without fire. And as the Fula nomads' proverb says, "At dawn you can already know if the day will be good or bad." Maybe my mind began to doubt the voice of duty, too well heeled, too well dressed to be honest. Maybe my mind was already preparing to say "no" to the inhuman laws that pass for humane. But I held on to hope, despite all her refusals, even if I knew, I understood why Fary always said "no" up until the night before we left for the war, Mademba and I.

XVI

GOD'S TRUTH, DOCTOR FRANÇOIS is a good man. Doctor François gives us time to think, to come back to ourselves. Doctor François gathers us, me and the others, in a big room where there are tables and chairs like at school. I've never been to school, but Mademba went. Mademba knew how to speak French, I don't. Doctor François is like a schoolmaster. He tells us to sit down on the chairs, and on each table his daughter, Mademoiselle François, dressed all in white, places a piece of paper and a pencil. Then, signing with his hands, Doctor François tells us to draw whatever we want. I know, I understand that behind the glasses that magnify his matching blue eyes, Doctor François is looking inside our heads. His matching blue eyes aren't like those of the enemies from the other side, who wanted to separate our heads from the rest of our bodies with their small malicious shells. His piercing, matching blue eyes are scrutinizing us in order to save our minds. I know, I understand that our drawings are there to help him wash our minds clean of the filth of war. I know, I understand that Doctor François is a purifier of heads that have been soiled by war.

God's truth, Doctor François is reserved. Doctor François almost never speaks to us. He only speaks to us with his eyes. That's convenient, because I don't know how to speak French, unlike Mademba, who went to the Toubabs' school. So I speak to Doctor François with my drawings. My drawings please Doctor François, who tells me so with his big matching blue eyes when he looks at me, smiling. Doctor François nods and I understand what he wants to say to me. He wants to say that what I am drawing is very beautiful and very expressive. I know, I understand very quickly that my drawings tell my story. I know, I understand that Doctor François reads my drawings like a story.

The first thing I drew on the piece of paper given to me by Doctor François was a woman's head. I drew my mother's head. God's truth, my mother is very beautiful in my memory and I drew her coiffed in the Fulani style, adorned with jewelry in the Fulani style. Doctor François was overcome by the beautiful details of my drawing. His big matching blue eyes behind his glasses clearly told me so. With nothing but my pencil, I brought my mother's head to life. I knew, I understood very quickly what brings a head drawn in pencil to life, in the portrait of a woman such as this one of my mother. What brings a drawing on a piece of paper to life is the play of shadow and light. I put some glints of light in my mother's big eyes. These glints of light leapt out from white slivers of paper that I had not colored in with black. Her head was also brought to life by minuscule slivers of paper that my pencil had barely touched with black. God's truth, I knew, I understood, I figured out how, with a simple pencil on paper, I could tell Doctor François how beautiful my Fula mother was, with heavy gold twists hanging from her ears and thin circles of red gold piercing the wings of her hooked nose. I could tell Doctor François how beautiful my mother was in my childhood memories, with her charcoaled eyelids, her painted lips half parted to reveal her beautiful, white, very, very well-aligned teeth, and with her head of hair threaded with gold. I drew her in shadows and light. God's truth, I believe that my drawing was so vivid, Doctor François heard my mother say from her sketched mouth that she was gone, but that she had not forgotten me. That she was gone and had left me with my father, the old man, but that she loved me still.

My mother was my father's fourth and final wife. My mother was a source of joy and then of pain for him. My mother was the only child of Yoro Ba. Yoro Ba was a Fula shepherd who walked his herd across my father's fields each year, during the migration south. His herd, which came from the Senegal River valley, was brought during the dry season to the eternally green plains of the Niayes, very close to Gandiol. Yoro Ba loved my father, the old man, because he gave him access to his artesian wells. God's truth, the peasants of Gandiol didn't like the Fula shepherds. But my father wasn't a peasant like the others. My father had opened a path in the middle of his fields toward his own wells just for Yoro Ba's herd. To those who wanted to know why, my father always said that everyone must live. My father had hospitality in his blood.

You don't give such a beautiful gift with impunity to a Fula worth his name. A Fula worth his name like Yoro Ba who drives his herd in the middle of my father's fields to give them water from his wells would have to give a very, very big gift in return. God's truth, my mother is the one who told me: a Fula who has been given a gift he can't return may die of shame. A Fula, she told me, is capable of stripping himself naked to pay a griot for a song if he has nothing left but his clothing to give. A Fula worthy of the name, she said to me, would even go so far as to cut off one of his ears to pay a traveling griot when he has nothing left but a piece of his body to give.

For Yoro Ba, who was a widower, apart from his herd of white, red, and black cows, what he valued most was his one daughter amid his five sons. God's truth, for Yoro Ba, his daughter, Penndo Ba, was without price. For Yoro Ba, his daughter deserved to marry a prince. Penndo could have earned him a regal dowry, at least a big herd equivalent to his, at least thirty camels from the northern Moors. God's truth, my mother told me this.

So Yoro Ba, because he was a Fula worthy of the name, announced to my father, the old man, that he would give him his daughter Penndo Ba's hand in marriage on the next transhumance. Yoro Ba asked no dowry for his daughter. He wanted only one thing: that my father would set a date for his marriage to Penndo. Yoro Ba paid for everything, he bought the bridal clothing and the twisted gold jewels, he slaughtered twenty heads of cattle from his own herd on the day of the wedding. He paid the singing griots with dozens of meters of expensive cloth, with heavy bazin brocade and lightweight indienne made in France.

You don't say "no" to a Fula worthy of the name who gives you his beloved daughter's hand in marriage as repayment for the hospitality shown to his herd. You can ask "why?" of a Fula worthy of the name, but you can't tell him "no." God's truth, my father did ask Yoro Ba, "Why?" and Yoro Ba answered, my mother told me this, "Bassirou Coumba Ndiaye, you are a simple peasant but you are noble. In the words of a Fula proverb: 'Until a man is dead, he is not yet done being created.' I have met many men in my life, but not a single man like you. I am learning from your wisdom, that I may grow in wisdom. Because you have shown the hospitality of a prince, when I give you my daughter, Penndo, I am mixing my blood with that of a king who does not know he is a king. In giving Penndo to you in marriage, I am reconciling immobility and mobility, the stillness of time and the flow of time, the past and the present. I am reconciling the rooted trees and the wind that rustles their leaves, the earth and the sky."

You can't say "no" to a Fula who gives you his own blood. So my father, the old man who already had three wives, said "yes" to the fourth, with the agreement of the three others. And this fourth wife, Penndo Ba, is the one who gave me life.

But seven years after Penndo Ba's wedding, six years after my birth, Yoro Ba, his five sons, and their herd stopped returning to Gandiol.

For the next two years Penndo Ba lived only for their return. The first year, Penndo remained amicable with her co-wives, with her husband, with me, her only child, but she was not happy. She didn't like staying in one place. Penndo had accepted my father, the old man, even though she had barely finished childhood. She agreed to marry him out of respect for keeping one's word, out of respect for Yoro Ba. Penndo had come to love my father because he was her exact opposite. He was as old as an immutable landscape, she was young like the changing sky. He was immobile as a baobab tree, she was the daughter of the wind. Sometimes opposites fascinate each other because of the differences between them. Penndo had come to love my father, the old man, because he contained all of the wisdom of the earth and of the recurring seasons. My father, the old man, idolized Penndo because she was what he was not: movement, joyous instability, novelty.

But Penndo couldn't handle immobility for seven years except on the condition that her father, her brothers, and their herd would return each year to see her at Gandiol. They brought with them the scent of travel, the scent of their encampments in the scrub brush, the scent of nights spent on guard to defend their herd from hungry lions. They brought in their eyes the memories of animals they had lost on the road and always found, living or dead, never abandoned. They told her of roads lost to the dust in daytime and rediscovered by starlight. In the singing language of the Fula people, they recounted their year of nomadic life each time they passed through Gandiol, driving their large herd of white, red, and black cows toward the eternally green plains of the Niayes.

Penndo, who could only survive Gandiol when she was able to look forward to their return, began to wither the very first year of their absence. Penndo Ba stopped laughing for good the second year they didn't come. Every morning during the dry season, when they should have been there, she would send me to go look at the well where Yoro Ba used to bring his herd to drink. She looked sadly at the path through the middle of the fields that my father had cut for them. She tilted her ear, hoping to hear the distant sound of Yoro Ba's animals and her brothers. I secretly watched her eyes, crazed with loneliness and regret, when we would return slowly to Gandiol after hours of unacknowledged waiting at the farthest northern border of the village.

I was nine years old when my father, who loved Penndo Ba, told her to leave to look for Yoro Ba, for her brothers and their herd. My father preferred her to leave than to die. I know, I understand that my father would rather have had my mother alive but far away from him than dead on his doorstep, laid to rest in the Gandiol cemetery. I know this, I understand it because my father became an old man as soon as Penndo left us. From one day to the next, his hair turned completely white. From one day to the next, his back hunched. From one day to the next, my father fell still. As soon as Penndo left, my father began to wait for her. God's truth, no one would have dreamed of mocking him for it.

Penndo wanted to bring me with her, but my father, the old man, refused. My father said that I was too young to leave on an adventure. It wouldn't be easy to find Yoro Ba while saddled with a young child. But I knew, I understood that in fact my father was afraid that Penndo would never return if I left with her. With me in Gandiol, he was assured she would have a very, very important reason to come home. God's truth, my father loved Penndo.

One evening, not long before her departure, Penndo Ba, my mother, took me in her arms. She said to me, in her musical language, Fulfulde, which I no longer understand, that I was a big boy, that I should be able to listen to her reasons. She needed to know what had happened to my grandfather, to my uncles and their herd. We never abandon those who gave us life. Once she knew, she would return: she would never abandon the one she had given life. God's truth, my mother's words both helped me and hurt me. She held me in her arms and she said nothing more. Like my father, as soon as she left I began to wait for her.

My father, the old man, had asked my older half brother, Ndiaga, the fisherman, to carry Penndo in his canoe as far as possible on the river north, then east. My mother asked for me to be able to accompany her for half the journey. Ndiaga had attached a smaller canoe to the back of the large one that carried me, my mother, and Saliou, another of my half brothers, who was to bring me back to Gandiol when the time came. Seated side by side on a bench at the head of the canoe, silent, we held hands, my mother and I. Together we looked at the river's horizon without really seeing it. From time to time the erratic swaying of the boat would deposit my head on Penndo's naked shoulder. I felt the flashes of her skin's heat against my right ear. Finally I attached myself to her arm so that my head no longer left her shoulder. I dreamed that the goddess Mame Coumba Bang would keep us in the middle of the river for a long time, despite the libations of cheese curd we'd offered her when we left the shores of our village. I prayed that she would entwine our canoe in her long liquid arms, that her brown algae hair would slow our progress despite the long paddle strokes my half brothers were using to beat her back so we could resist her powerful current. Out of breath from their river-peasant labors tracing invisible grooves in the water, Ndiaga and Saliou were silent. They were as sad for me as they were for my mother, who was about to be separated from her only son. God's truth, even my half brothers loved Penndo Ba.

The time came for us to separate. Mute, head and eyes lowered, we stretched our joined hands toward my mother so she could bless us. We listened to her murmur unfamiliar prayers, long prayers of blessing from a Koran she knew better than we did. When she fell quiet, we raised the palms of our joined hands to our faces, to collect every last breath of her prayers, as if we were drinking from their source. Then Saliou and I moved into the small canoe, which Ndiaga had cut free with an abrupt gesture filled with suppressed anger directed at himself, at the tears that were rising to fill his eyes. Then my mother looked at me intensely one last time to cement my image in her memory. And then, as my canoe was carried in the soft lapping of the current, she turned her back. I know, I understand that she didn't want me to see her cry. God's truth, a Fula woman worthy of the name does not cry in front of her son. But I cried very, very much.

No one really knows what happened to Penndo Ba. My half brother Ndiaga brought her by canoe as far as the city of Saint-Louis. There, he entrusted her to another fisherman by the name of Sadibou Guèye, who was to take her for the price of a sheep in his commercial canoe as far as Walaldé, in Diéri, the usual camping spot at this time of the year for Yoro Ba, his five sons, and their herd. But the waters of the river were too low, and Sadibou Guèye passed Penndo on to one of his cousins, Badara Diaw, so that he could accompany her along the riverbank on foot as far as Walaldé. Very few people reported seeing them beyond the village of Mboyo, after which they evaporated into the brush. My mother and Badara Diaw never made it to Walaldé.

God's truth, we learned this when my father, after a year, tired of waiting for news of Penndo and Yoro Ba, sent my half brother Ndiaga to question Sadibou Guèye, who on a moment's notice traveled to Podor, where Badara Diaw lived. Badara Diaw's family had already, after a month without news of him, researched the route that he had told them he was taking with my mother. Weeping tears of blood, they told Sadibou Guèye what they feared had happened. Surely Badara and Penndo had both been kidnapped, just outside Mboyo, by a dozen Moorish horsemen, the traces of whom villagers had noticed on the riverbanks. The Moors from the north would kidnap black people to make slaves of them. I know, I understand that when they saw Penndo Ba's beauty they did not hesitate to take her to sell her to their great sheikh for the price of thirty camels. I know, I understand that they captured her travel companion, Badara Diaw, too so that her theft would go unavenged.

As soon as he learned the news of Penndo Ba's capture by the Moors, my father passed definitively into old age. God's truth, he continued to laugh, to smile at us, to joke about the world and about himself, but he was never the same again. In one instant he had lost half of his youth, he had lost half of his joy in existing.

XVII

THE SECOND DRAWING I made for Doctor François was a portrait of Mademba, my friend, my more-than-brother. This drawing was less beautiful. Not because it was less successful, but because Mademba was ugly. I still think so, even if it isn't completely true, because, despite the fact that death now separates us, the history of our teasing survives between us. But if Mademba wasn't as beautiful as I am on the outside, inside he was more so.

When my mother left and didn't come back, Mademba

took me in. He took me by the hand and led me into his parents' compound. My move into Mademba's house happened slowly, over time. I slept there one night, then two in a row, then three. God's truth, my installment in Mademba Diop's family took place gradually. I no longer had my maman. Mademba, who felt my pain more than anyone else in Gandiol, wanted his maman to adopt me. Mademba took me by the hand and led me to Aminata Sarr: he put my hand into his mother's and said, "I want Alfa Ndiaye to live with us, I want you to become his maman." My father's other wives weren't mean, they were even nice to me, especially the first one, Ndiaga and Saliou's mother. But despite that, I gradually left my family to join Mademba's. My father, the old man, accepted it without a word. He said "yes" to Aminata Sarr, Mademba's mother, when she asked to adopt me. Every year during the Tabaski Festival, my father even asked his first wife, Aïda Mbengue, to give the best part of the sacrificial sheep to Aminata Sarr. He ended up giving an entire sacrificial sheep to Mademba's family. My father, the old man, could no longer look at me without wanting to cry. I knew, I understood that I resembled his Penndo too much.

Gradually the sadness left, gradually Aminata Sarr and Mademba, aided by the passage of time, made me forget the gnawing pain. At first, Mademba and I would go off to play in the brush, always heading north. He and I knew, between ourselves, we understood why. But we kept our hopes quiet, that we would be the first to see my mother, Yoro Ba, his five sons, and their herd. What we told Aminata Sarr about our daylong expeditions to the north was that they were to catch palm rats in traps, or to hunt turtledoves with slingshots. She would give us her blessing and a few provisions, three pinches of salt and a flask of cold water. And whenever we caught palm rats or turtledoves and roasted them—after gutting, plucking, or butchering them—staked on dry branches, we would forget my mother, her father, her five brothers, and their herd. Watching the orange flames of our small fire sizzle, reanimated from time to time by fat oozing from the crackling flesh of our haul from the brush, we were no longer thinking about the pain of absence that wrung our guts, but of the hunger that wrung them just as much. We stopped dreaming that by some incredible miracle Penndo had escaped her Moorish captors, that she had reunited in Walaldé with her father, her five brothers, and their herd, and that they would return together to Gandiol. At that moment, so close to her kidnapping, the only way I knew to surmount the irreversible absence of my mother was by hunting and cooking palm rats and turtledoves with Mademba, my more-than-brother.

We grew up, gradually, Mademba and I. And gradually we stopped taking the road north from Gandiol to wait for Penndo to return. At fifteen, we were circumcised on the same day. We were initiated into the secrets of adulthood by the same village elder. He explained to us how to conduct ourselves. The greatest secret he taught us was that it isn't the man who controls events but events that control the man. Any event that surprises a man has already been experienced by other men before him. The effects of all human possibilities have already been felt. Nothing that might happen to us here, as terrible or as felicitous as it might seem, is new. But what we experience is always new because every man is unique, the way every leaf and every tree is unique. Men share with each other the same lifeblood, but each feeds himself from it differently. Even if the new isn't really new, it's always new for those who, ceaselessly, wash up on the world's shores, generation after generation, wave after wave. So, in order to find yourself in life, to not lose yourself on the path, you must listen to the voice of duty. To think too much about yourself is to falter. Whoever understands this secret has the potential to live in peace. But it's easier said than done.

I became tall and strong and Mademba remained short and frail. Every year in the dry season, the desire to see Penndo would take me by the throat again. I didn't know how to chase my mother from my mind except by exhausting my body. I worked in my father's fields and in those of Siré Diop, Mademba's father. I danced, I swam, I wrestled, while Mademba sat and studied, and studied more. God's truth, Mademba learned the holy book like no one else in

Gandiol. By the age of twelve he could recite the Holy Koran by heart, while I could barely recite my prayers at fifteen. Once he had become more knowledgeable than our marabout, Mademba wanted to go to the white school. Siré Diop, who didn't want his son to remain a peasant like him, agreed on the condition that I go with him. During those years, I would escort him to the threshold of the school, which I only crossed once. Nothing could enter into the insides of my head. I know, I understand that the memory of my mother had calcified the entire surface of my mind so it was hard like a tortoise's shell. I know, I understand that there was nothing beneath this shell but the void of waiting. God's truth, the space where knowledge would have gone was already occupied. So I preferred to work in the field, to dance and wrestle to prove the extent of my powers, to not think about the impossible return of my mother, Penndo Ba. It was only once Mademba was dead that my mind opened enough to let me see what was hiding there. You might say that with Mademba's death, a big metal seed of war fell from the sky and cracked my mind's shell in two. God's truth, a new suffering joined with the old one. The two contemplated each other, they explained each other, they gave each other meaning.

When we turned twenty, Mademba wanted to go to war. School had put it in his head that he should save the motherland, France. Mademba wanted to become a somebody in

Saint-Louis, a French citizen: "Alfa, the world is big, I want to see it. The war is a chance to leave Gandiol. God willing, we will return safe and sound. When we become French citizens, we'll move to Saint-Louis. We'll start a business. We'll become wholesalers and we'll distribute food to the shops in northern Senegal, including the ones in Gandiol! Once we're rich, we'll look for and find your mother, and we'll buy her back from the Moorish horsemen who took her." I bought into his dream. God's truth, I owed him. And yet I said to myself that if I also became a somebody, a Senegalese rifleman for life, it could be that in the company of my detail I might one day visit the tribes of the northern Moors with my regulation rifle in my left hand and my savage machete in my right.

At first the recruiters told Mademba "no." Mademba was too frail, as light and delicate as a crowned crane. Mademba was not suited to war. But God's truth, Mademba was stubborn. Mademba, who to that point was only resistant to mental fatigue, asked me to help him become resistant to physical fatigue. So, for two whole months, I forced Mademba's feeble strength to grow and grow. I made him run in the heavy sand beneath the leaden midday sun, I made him swim across the river, I made him swing a daba in his father's fields for hours and hours. God's truth, I forced him to eat enormous quantities of boiled millet mixed with hot milk and peanut butter, as fighters worthy of the name do to put on weight.

The second time, the recruiting soldiers said "yes." They didn't recognize him. He had gone from crowned crane to fat partridge. For Doctor François, I drew the laugh that sprang to Mademba Diop's face when I explained to him that if he wanted to become a wrestler he already had an alias: Turtle-dove Chest! I drew, in shadows and light, how Mademba's eyes creased with laugher when I added that he'd puffed out so much his own totem wouldn't recognize him.

XVIII

THE NIGHT BEFORE WE LEFT for the war in France, Fary Thiam said "yes" to me with her eyes, discreetly, surrounded by the girls and boys of our age set. It was a full moon that night, we were twenty years old and we wanted to laugh. We told each other short sweet stories full of innuendo, and riddles too. We weren't gathered in Mademba's parents' compound that evening, as we were four years before. Mademba's younger brothers and sisters had gotten too old to sleep through our suggestive stories. We were seated on wide mats on the corner of a sandy street in the village, sheltered by the low branches of a mango tree. Fary was more beautiful than ever in a saffron yellow dress that clung to her chest, her waist and hips. In the moonlight, her dress looked pure white. Fary shot me a quick but loaded look that seemed to say, "Get ready, Alfa, something important is going to happen!" Fary took my hand as she had on the night when she chose me when we were sixteen years old, glanced surreptitiously at the middle of my body, then got up and left the group. I waited until she'd disappeared around the corner and I got up as well to follow her from a distance to the small ebony forest, where we weren't afraid to see the river goddess Mame Coumba Bang because of the desire we felt, my desire to enter the depths of Fary's body, hers for me to enter it.

I know, I understand why Fary Thiam opened the inside of her body to me before we left for the war, Mademba and I. The inside of Fary's body was warm, soft, and moist. I had never tasted, with my mouth or with my skin, anything so warm, soft, and moist as the interior of Fary Thiam's body. The part of my body, my inside-outside, that entered Fary had never received such an enveloping embrace from top to bottom, neither in the hot sand on the shores of the ocean where, flat on my stomach, I had often thrust it for my own pleasure, nor in the secret of river water beneath my soapy hands' caress. God's truth, I had never known anything better in my life than the tender moist heat of the inside of Fary's body, and I know, I understand why she let me taste it though it ruined her family's honor.

I think Fary began to think for herself before I did. I think she wanted a body as beautiful as mine to know this sweet happiness before disappearing into the war. I know, I understand that Fary wanted to make me a man before I went to offer my beautiful body to the bloody battlefields of war. This is why Fary offered herself to me despite the ancestral prohibition. God's truth, my body had experienced all sorts of great joys before Fary. I had felt its power in back-to-back wrestling matches, I had pushed it to the edges of its resistance in long races on the beach after swimming across the river. I had sprayed it with seawater beneath a sun as hot as hell, I had quenched it with cold water drawn from the deep wells of Gandiol after swinging a daba in my father's and Siré Diop's fields for hours and hours. God's truth, my body had known the pleasure of reaching the limits of its power, but never had anything been as powerful as Fary's warm, soft, and moist interior. God's truth, Fary offered me the most beautiful present a young woman could offer a young man on the eve of his departure for war. To die without knowing all of the pleasures of the body isn't fair. God's truth, I know with certainty that Mademba never experienced the pleasure of entering the insides of a woman's body. I know it, he died even though he wasn't a man yet.

He would have become one if he had known the tender, wet, and soft sweetness of the interior of a woman he loved. Poor, incomplete Mademba.

I know, I understand the other reason Fary Thiam opened the inside of her body to me before we left for the war, Mademba and I. When rumors about the war arrived in the village, Fary understood very well that France and its army would take me from her. She knew, she understood that I would be leaving forever. She knew, she understood that even if I didn't die at war, I would never return to Gandiol. She knew, she understood that I would settle in Saint-Louis du Senegal with Mademba Diop, that I would want to become a somebody, a Senegalese rifleman for life, with a big pension to make my old father's final years easier, and to one day reunite with my mother, Penndo Ba. Fary Thiam understood that France would take me from her, whether I lived or died.

That's the other reason Fary offered me the warm, sweet, and wet insides of her body before I left to make war with the Toubabs, despite the honor of the Thiam family, despite the hatred her father felt for mine.

XIX III

ABDOU THIAM IS THE VILLAGE CHIEF of Gandiol. This was determined by traditional law. Abdou Thiam detests my father because my father, the old man, made him lose face in front of everyone. Abdou Thiam collects the village taxes and one day he convened an assembly of the elders, which was soon joined by all the people of Gandiol. Inspired by a king's envoy from Cayor and incited by a governor's envoy from Saint-Louis, Abdou Thiam said that we needed to follow a new path, that we needed to cultivate peanuts instead of millet, peanuts instead of tomatoes, peanuts instead of onions, peanuts instead of cabbage, peanuts instead of watermelons. Peanuts meant more money for everyone. Peanuts meant more money to pay taxes. Peanuts would give new nets to the fishermen. Peanuts meant new wells could be dug. The money from the peanuts would mean brick houses, a permanent school, corrugated metal roofs for our huts. The money from the peanuts would mean trains and roads, motors on our canoes, clinics and maternity wards. Those who farmed peanuts, Chief Abdou Thiam concluded, would be exempt from their corvées, from mandatory labor. Those who didn't would not.

So my father, the old man, stood up and asked permission to speak. I am his youngest son, his youngest child. My father has worn a helmet of white hair on his head since Penndo Ba left us. My father is a soldier of everyday life who only lived to protect his wives and his children from hunger. Day after day, in the river of time that is life, my father filled our bellies with the fruits of his fields and his orchards. My father, the old man, made us, his family, grow stronger and more beautiful just like the plants he fed to us. He was a grower of trees and fruits, he was a grower of children. We grew tall and strong like the seeds he planted in the loamy soils of his fields.

My father, the old man, stood up and asked permission to speak. It was granted, and he said:

"I, Bassirou Coumba Ndiaye, the grandson of Sidy Mal-
amine Ndiaye, the great-grandson of the grandson of one of
the five founders of our village, I am going to tell you, Abdou
Thiam, something that you will not like. I will not refuse to
dedicate one of my fields to the cultivation of peanuts, but
I refuse to dedicate all of my fields to peanuts. Peanuts cannot feed my family. Abdou Thiam, you say that peanuts are
money, but God's truth, I don't need money. I feed my family with millet, tomatoes, onions, red beans, with the watermelons that grow in my fields. I have a cow that gives me
milk, I have a few sheep that give me meat. One of my sons
who is a fisherman gives me dried fish. My wives extract salt
from the soil all year long. With all of this food I can even
open my doors to a hungry traveler, I can perform the sacred
duty of hospitality.

"But if I only grow peanuts, what will feed my family?
Who will feed the passing travelers who deserve my hospitality? Money from peanuts can't feed them all. Tell me, Abdou
Thiam, would I not be forced to come to your store to buy
food? Abdou Thiam, you will not like what I am going to say
to you, but a village chief should concern himself with the
people's interests before his own. Abdou Thiam, you and I
are equals and I do not want, one day, to have to come to your
store to beg for rice on credit, for oil on credit, for sugar on
credit to feed my own. I also do not want to close my door to
a hungry traveler because I myself am hungry.

"Abdou Thiam, you won't like what I'm going to say, but the day when all of the villages in our area only cultivate peanuts, the price of peanuts will go down. We will earn less and less money and you yourself will end up having to live on credit. A shopkeeper whose clients are all debtors becomes himself a debtor to his suppliers.

"Abdou Thiam, you won't like what I'm going to say. I, Bassirou Coumba Ndiaye, remember the year we call 'the year of hunger.' Your late grandfather might have spoken to you about it. It was the year after the locusts came, the year of the great drought, the year the wells dried up, the year the dust blew down from the north, the year the river was too low to irrigate our fields. I was a young child but I remember that if we had not all shared everything during that infernally dry year, if we hadn't shared our stores of millet, of red beans, our stores of onions, of cassava, if we hadn't shared our milk and our sheep, we would all have died. Abdou Thiam, peanuts wouldn't have saved us then, and the money from peanuts wouldn't have saved us either. To survive the devil's drought, we would surely have eaten the seed peanuts for the following year's crop and we would have had to buy more on credit from the same people we'd sold our crop to at whatever price they set. From that moment on, we would have been poor forever, beggars forever! That is why, Abdou Thiam, even if you won't like it, I say 'no' to peanuts and I say 'no' to peanut money!"

My father's speech didn't please Abdou Thiam one bit—he was very, very angry, but he didn't show it. Abdou Thiam didn't like it that my father said he was a bad chief. Abdou Thiam didn't like it one bit that someone had mentioned his shop. So, the last thing in the world that Abdou Thiam would have wanted was for his daughter Fary to get together with one of Bassirou Coumba Ndiaye's sons. Fary Thiam gave herself to me in the small ebony forest before I left for war in France. Fary loved me more than the honor of her father, who had none.

XX ııı

THE THIRD THING I DREW for Doctor François was my seven hands. I drew them so that I could really see them, the way they were when I cut them off. I was curious to find out how the shadow and light, the paper and pencil, would allow me to reproduce them, if they would come to life before my eyes as fully as my mother's head, or Mademba's. The result surpassed my expectations. God's truth, when I saw them I could have believed that they'd just now been greasing, loading, firing the rifles that they held before my machete separated them from the arms of the men I tortured in no-man's-land. I drew them one next to the other on the big white page that Mademoiselle François had given me. God's truth, I even took care to draw each hair on their backs, their black nails, the more or less successful cuts across their wrists.

I was very pleased with myself. I should say that I was no longer in possession of my seven hands. God's truth, I'd thought it more reasonable to get rid of them. And by then Doctor François had already begun to wash the filth of war from inside my head. My seven hands were fury, were vengeance, were the madness of war. I no longer wanted to see the fury and the madness of war, the same way my captain could no longer tolerate seeing my seven hands in the trench. So one evening I decided to bury them. God's truth, I waited for the night of a full moon to do it. I know, I understand that I shouldn't have buried them on the night of a full moon. I know, I understand that they could have spotted me from the west wing of our sanctuary while I was digging in the dirt to bury them. But I thought that I owed a burial under a full moon to the men I'd tortured in no-man's-land. I had killed them with the complicity of the moon. The moon hid itself in order to conceal me from their eyes. They died in the shadows of no-man's-land. They deserved a bit of light.

I know, I understand that I shouldn't have, because once

I'd finished burying them, neatly arranged in a box sealed with my mystical padlock, as I returned to the sanctuary, I thought I saw a shadow slipping behind one of the big windows in the west wing. I know, I understand that someone from the sanctuary must have discovered my secret. It's why I waited a few days before drawing my hands. I waited to see if someone would report me. But nobody said anything. So, to cleanse the insides of my head with big buckets of mystical water, I drew my seven hands. I had to show them to Doctor François so that they would leave the inside of my head.

My seven hands spoke, they confessed all to my judges. God's truth, I know, I understand that my drawings denounced me. After seeing them, Doctor François no longer smiled at me like before.

XXI ₁₁₁

WHERE AM I? It feels like I've returned from far away. Who am I? I don't know anymore. Shadows surround me, I can't see anything, but I begin to sense a warmth lending me life. I try to open eyes that aren't mine, to move hands that don't belong to me, but that will belong to me soon, I can tell. My legs are there . . . Strange, I feel something beneath my dream of a body. There, where I'm returning from, I swear to you, all is immobile. There where I've come from, there is no body. But, now, I who was nowhere, I sense myself living. I sense myself becoming incarnate. I sense flesh, bathed in red-hot blood, enclose me. I sense against my belly, against my soon-to-be chest, another body moving, infusing mine with heat. I feel it warming my skin. Where I've come from, there is no heat. Where I've come from, I swear, nobody has a name. I'm going to open my eyes that are no longer mine. I don't know who I am. My name escapes me still, but I'll remember it soon. Strange, the body beneath mine isn't moving anymore. Strange, I sense its immobile heat beneath me. Strange, I sense, suddenly, hands pressing on my back, a back that doesn't entirely belong to me yet, thighs that are not yet mine, a neck that doesn't belong to me but that I absorb, that I accept as mine, thanks to the soft hands touching me. Strange, the hands are suddenly pummeling my back, my thighs, scratching at my neck. Beneath their scratching, this body that wasn't yet mine became mine. I swear to you, it's pleasant to leave nothingness. I swear to you that I was there without being there.

And now it's done: I have my body. For the first time I have come inside a woman. I swear to you, it's the first time. I swear to you that it's very, very good. Before now I had never come in the insides of a woman because I didn't have a body. A voice from very, very far away said to me, "It's much better than with your hand!" This voice from far away whispers in my head, "It's as loud as the first shell exploding on a silent morning, it wrenches your guts." It's the voice from far away that tells me again, "There's nothing better in the world." I know, I understand that it's this voice from far away that will give me a name. I know, I understand, the voice will soon baptize me.

The woman who has given me this bodily pleasure is beneath me. She is immobile, her eyes closed. I swear to you that I don't know her, I've never seen her. In fact, she's the one who gave me eyes to see by offering herself to my view. I swear to you that I see with eyes that aren't mine, that I touch with hands that don't belong to me. It's incredible, but I swear to you that it's the truth. My inside-outside, as the voice from far away calls it, is now in an unknown woman's body. I can feel the interior heat of this woman's body, surrounding it from top to bottom. I swear to you that I feel as if I'm inhabiting my own body now that I've inhabited the body of the unknown woman. She lies beneath me, she isn't moving, her eyes are closed, I don't know who she is. I swear to you that I don't know why she agreed to welcome my inside-outside into her interior. It's unusual to find yourself lying on top of an unknown woman. It's unusual to have the impression of being a stranger in your own body.

Even my hands I'm seeing for the first time. I shake them, I move them across both sides of the head of this woman I am lying on top of. Her eyes are closed. I am leaning on my elbows. I sense her breasts brushing against my chest.

I observe my two hands trembling near her head. I didn't think they'd be so big. I swear to you that I thought I had smaller hands, thinner fingers. I don't know why, but here I am with very, very large hands. It's strange, but when I bend my fingers, when I clench and unclench my fists, I can tell that I have the hands of a wrestler. I swear to you that where I come from I didn't seem to have a wrestler's hands. The little voice from far away is what told me that from now on I would possess a wrestler's hands. This is a surprise. I have to find out if the rest of my body is the body of a wrestler. I have to verify the state of this body that is mine without being mine. I have to detach my body from the unknown woman who lies beneath me. She seems to be sleeping. It's strange that I don't look at her very much, although she's beautiful—I get the sense that I like beautiful women. But first I have to look again at my body to find out if it resembles a wrestler's body, as the voice from far away claims.

I detach myself from this beautiful woman with her eyes closed who is lying beneath me. It's strange to hear the sound of our two bodies detaching. I want to laugh. It makes a small moist sound like that of a child pulling his thumb out of his mouth quickly because his mother has forbidden him to suck on it. This image that comes from far away makes me laugh inside my head. It's also strange to find myself lying next to an unknown woman. Not to mention that it's strange to feel my heart beating so fast in my excitement to find out if the rest of my body is like my hands. I lift my arms toward the ceiling of the white bedroom. My two arms: I swear to you, they're like two old mango tree trunks. I rest my arms alongside my body. I lift my two legs straight at the ceiling of the white room: I swear to you, you would say they look like two baobab tree trunks. I stretch my two legs out again on the bed and I say to myself that it's strange to find oneself in the body of a wrestler. It's strange to arrive in the world in such good physical condition. It's strange to discover that you have such strength. I swear to you that I don't have any fear of the unknown, I fear nothing, just like a real wrestler, but it's still strange to be born in a beautiful wrestler's body next to a beautiful woman instead of in the body of a weakling lying next to an ugly one.

I am not afraid of the unknown. I swear to you. I'm not even afraid not to know my own name. My body tells me that I'm a wrestler and that's enough. No need to know my name, my body is enough. No need to know where I am, my body is enough. No need for anything from now on except to explore the power of my new body. Once again, I lift my arms, thick as mature mango tree trunks, toward the ceiling of the white room. My hands seem farther from my shoulders than I expected. I clench my fists, then I unclench them, I clench and unclench them again. It's strange to see the muscles in my arms dance beneath my skin. My arms are heavier than I expected, they're full of a suppressed power that feels like it could explode at any moment. But I'm not afraid of the unknown.

XXII ₪

THANK YOU, MADEMOISELLE FRANÇOIS! God's truth, I am not mistaken. Even if I don't speak French, I know, I understand the meaning of Mademoiselle François's eyes sweeping across the middle of my body. Mademoiselle François is unsurpassed when it comes to speaking with her eyes. Her eyes told me very clearly that I should appear in her room the evening of the day they swept across the middle of my body.

Her bedroom was at the end of a corridor painted in a

white so bright that it gleamed in the fiery moonlight behind each of the windows I silently passed. It was absolutely necessary that Doctor François not know that I was going to visit his daughter. It was also absolutely necessary that the guard from the west wing of the sanctuary not see me. The door to her room was open. When I entered, Mademoiselle François was asleep. I lay down next to her. Mademoiselle François woke up and she cried out because she didn't know that I was me. I placed my left hand on Mademoiselle François's mouth, which fought and fought. But, as the captain said, I am a force of nature. I waited to make sure Mademoiselle François was no longer moving before I lifted my hand from her mouth. Mademoiselle François smiled at me. So I smiled at her too. Thank you, Mademoiselle François, for opening your little notch, so close to your guts. God's truth, vive la guerre! God's truth, I plunged into her the way one plunges into the powerful current of a river one wants to cross, swimming furiously. God's truth, I thrust into her womb as if to disembowel her. God's truth, I tasted blood in my mouth, all of a sudden. God's truth, I didn't understand why.

XXIII_{III}

THEY ASK ME MY NAME, but I'm waiting for them to reveal it to me. I swear to you that I no longer know who I am. I can only tell them what I feel. I believe from looking at my arms like mango trees and my legs like baobabs that I am a great destroyer of life. I swear to you that I get the sense nothing can resist me, that I am immortal, that I could pulverize boulders just by squeezing them in my arms. I swear to you that what I'm feeling can't be said simply: the words with which I could say it are insufficient. So I resort to words that might seem foreign to what I want to say because at least, by chance, despite what they ordinarily signify, they might translate what it is I feel. For the moment I am only what my body feels. My body is trying to speak through my mouth. I don't know who I am, but I think I know what my body would say about me. The thickness of my body, its excessive power, can only bring combat to the minds of others, can only bring battle, war, violence, and death. My body accuses my body. But why is it that my body's bulk and its excessive power can't also mean peace, tranquility, and calm?

A small voice from very, very far away tells me that my body is the body of a wrestler. I swear to you that I only knew one wrestler in the world before. I don't remember his name. This big body that I've found myself in without knowing who I am is his, possibly. Possibly, he abandoned it to let me take his place, out of friendship, out of compassion. This is what's whispered to me by the small distant voice in my head.

XXIV.

"I AM THE SHADOW THAT DEVOURS ROCKS, mountains, forests, and rivers, the flesh of beasts and of men. I slice skin, I empty skulls and bodies. I cut off arms, legs, and hands. I smash bones and I suck out their marrow. But I am also the red moon that rises over the river, I am the evening air that rustles the tender acacia trees. I am the wasp and the flower. I am as much the wriggling fish as the still canoe, as much the net as the fisherman. I am the prisoner and his guard. I am the tree and the seed that grew into it. I am father and son. I am assassin and judge. I am the sowing and the harvest. I am mother and daughter. I am night and day. I am fire and the wood it devours. I am innocent and guilty. I am the beginning and the end. I am the creator and the destroyer. I am double."

To translate is never simple. To translate is to betray at the borders, it's to cheat, it's to trade one sentence for another. To translate is one of the only human activities in which one is required to lie about the details to convey the truth at large. To translate is to risk understanding better than others that the truth about a word is not single, but double, even triple, quadruple, or quintuple. To translate is to distance oneself from God's truth, which, as everyone knows or believes, is single.

"What did he say?" everyone asked. "This is not the response we expected. The response we expected wouldn't be more than two words, possibly three. Everyone has a last name and a first name, two first names at most."

The translator hesitated, intimidated by the angry, worried looks being shot his way. He cleared his throat and answered the uniforms in a small, nearly inaudible voice:

"He said that he is both death and life."

XXV <small>III</small>

SINCE THEN, I BELIEVE I KNOW who I am. I swear to you, God's truth, that the little voice entering my head from very, very far away helped me to guess. The little voice knew that my body couldn't reveal everything about me to me. God's truth, the little voice understood that my body was ambivalent about me. I swear to you that my body without scars is a strange body. Wrestlers, warriors have scars. I swear to you, God's truth, that the body of a wrestler without scars is not a normal body. That means that my body can't tell my story. It also means that my body, and it's the little voice from very, very far away that says so, is the body of a dëmm. The body of a devourer of souls has a good chance of being free of scars.

Everyone knows the story of the prince who came from nowhere to marry the fickle daughter of a vain king. The little voice that comes to my head from very, very far away recalls it. The fickle daughter of the vain king wanted a man without scars. She wanted a man without history.

The prince who came out of the brush to marry her didn't bear a single scar. This prince was terribly beautiful and the fickle princess liked him, but the princess's nurse did not. The princess's nurse knew, understood at first glance, that the terribly beautiful prince was a sorcerer. She knew it, she understood it precisely because he didn't have a single scar. Princes, like wrestlers, always have scars. It's their scars that tell their story. Princes, like wrestlers, must have at least one scar so that they can be turned into stories by their people. No scar, no epic. No scar, no great name. No scar, no renown. That's why the little voice in my head had to take matters in hand. That's why the little voice helped me guess my name. Because the body that I'm in, the body that was bequeathed to me, doesn't bear a single scar.

The fickle princess's nurse knew, she understood that the prince without scars was unnameable. The nurse warned the fickle princess of the nameless danger. But in vain. The fickle princess wanted her man without scars, she wanted her man without a story. So the nurse gave the fickle princess three talismans, saying, "Here is an egg, here is a bit of wood, and here is a pebble. When the day comes that you will be pursued by a great danger, throw them one after the other over your left shoulder. They will save you."

After her marriage to the terribly beautiful prince who'd come straight from the brush, it was time for her to leave for her bridegroom's kingdom. But her bridegroom's kingdom was distant and unknown. The farther the fickle princess went from her village, the more the prince's entourage dwindled, as if absorbed into the brush. As they vanished, each reverted to its true appearance, one a hare, one an elephant, one a hyena, one a peacock, one a black or green snake, one a crowned crane, one a dung beetle. But the prince, her terribly beautiful spouse, was a sorcerer, as the nurse had guessed. A lion-sorcerer who enslaved her for a long time in a forsaken cave in the brush.

The fickle princess bitterly regretted not having listened to the voice of her nurse, the voice of wisdom, the voice of warning. The fickle princess found herself in the middle of nowhere. She was in a place without a name, where the sand only looked like sand, where shrubs resembled shrubs, the sky, sky; a place where everything confused itself for everything else, a place where the ground too bore no scars, a place where the ground had no story.

So, as soon as she could, the fickle princess fled, but the lion-sorcerer took off after her in hot pursuit. The lion-sorcerer knew that if he lost the princess he would lose his only story, he would lose his meaning, he would lose even his name, that of lion-sorcerer. With the princess gone, his land became no-man's-land again, for it was the princess who had enlivened it with her fancies. His land would never resuscitate itself unless the fickle princess returned to his cave-kingdom. Even the life of the lion-sorcerer himself depended on the fickle princess's eyes, ears, and mouth. Without her, his scarless beauty would remain invisible, without her presence his roars would be inaudible, without her voice his cave-kingdom would be erased from the world.

The first time he almost caught her, she threw her nurse's egg over her left shoulder and it became an immense river. The fickle princess believed she had saved herself, but the lion-sorcerer drank all the water in the river. The second time he was on the point of capturing her, she threw the nurse's little stick over her left shoulder. It turned into an impenetrable forest, but the lion-sorcerer managed to cut it down, to uproot it. When the lion-sorcerer was, for the third time, at the point of catching her, the fickle princess could almost see the village of her father and her nurse. She threw the last talisman over her left shoulder, the small pebble, which transformed into a high mountain that the lion-sorcerer scaled and descended in giant leaps. Despite this final obstacle, the lion-sorcerer was still on the princess's trail. She didn't dare turn around, for fear of bringing the image of a far-off danger near. She could hear the rhythm of his steps beating the ground. Did the man-animal run on two legs or on four paws? She thought she could hear him pant. She could still smell his scent—of river, of forest, and of mountain, of a beast or a man who has survived the impossible. A hunter carrying a bow and arrows emerged from nowhere. The lion-sorcerer leapt on the fickle princess and was killed by an arrow straight to his heart. It was the first and the last wound for the lion-sorcerer. It's the reason we can tell his story.

When the lion-sorcerer fell in a cloud of yellow dust, you could hear a terrible sound growling from the depths of the brush. The ground trembled, daylight flickered. The cave-kingdom, kingdom of the inside of the earth, rose into the sunlight. Tall cliffs crashed into the heart of the lion-sorcerer's unnameable kingdom. Everyone could see the cliffs that rose into the sky from the brush. The cave-kingdom could thereafter be located by these giant raised scars in the earth. They are why we can now tell the kingdom's story.

The hunter-savior was the only son of the nurse who had offered the three talismans. The hunter-savior was ugly, the hunter-savior was poor, but he had saved the fickle princess.

In compensation for his bravery, the vain king married his fickle daughter to this hunter-savior who was covered with scars. He was a man with stories.

I SWEAR TO you that I heard the story of the lion-sorcerer just before leaving for the war. This story, like all interesting stories, is full of clever innuendo. Whoever tells a well-known story like the one about the lion-sorcerer and the fickle princess might always be hiding another story beneath it. To be seen, the story hidden beneath the well-known story has to peek out a little bit. If the hidden story hides too well beneath the well-known story, it stays invisible. The hidden story has to be there without being there, it has to let itself be guessed at, the way a tight saffron-yellow dress lets the beautiful figure of a young girl be guessed at. It has to be transparent. When it's understood by those for whom it is intended, the story hidden beneath the well-known story can change the course of their lives, can push them to transform a diffuse desire into a concrete act. It can heal them from the sickness of hesitation, no matter the expectations of an ill-intentioned storyteller.

I swear to you that I heard the story of the lion-sorcerer at night, seated on a mat spread out on white sand, in the company of the young boys and girls in my age set, beneath the protection of the low branches of a mango tree.

I swear to you that, like all of us who heard the story of the scarless lion-sorcerer that night, I knew, I understood that Fary Thiam had taken him for herself. I knew, I understood when Fary Thiam took her leave of us. I knew, I understood that Fary was daring anyone to think of her as a fickle princess. I knew, I understood that she wanted the lion-sorcerer. When Alfa Ndiaye, my more-than-brother, the man with the lion as a totem, got up too, so soon after Fary, I knew, I understood that he was going to join her in the brush. I knew, I understood that Alfa and Fary would find each other in the small ebony forest not far from the river of fire. There, Fary gave herself to Alfa before the two of us left the next morning for war in France. I know it because I was there without being there.

But now that I think deeply about it, now that I take on God's truth as my own, I know, I understand that Alfa left me a place in his wrestler's body out of friendship, out of compassion. I know, I understand that Alfa heard the first supplication I uttered in the depths of no-man's-land on the night of my death. Because I didn't want to be left alone in the middle of nowhere, in a land without a name. God's truth, I swear to you that now, whenever I think of us, he is me and I am him.

A NOTE ABOUT THE AUTHOR

David Diop was born in Paris and raised in Senegal. He is a professor at the University of Pau and Pays de l'Adour, where his research includes such topics as eighteenth-century French literature and European representations of Africa in the seventeenth and eighteenth centuries. *At Night All Blood Is Black* is his second novel.

A NOTE ABOUT THE TRANSLATOR

Anna Moschovakis has translated books by Albert Cossery, Annie Ernaux, Robert Bresson, and Marcelle Sauvageot, among others. Her novel *Eleanor, or The Rejection of the Progress of Love* was published in 2018.